THE IDIO

AT

To
Florence

Enjoy!

A Stammans.

THE IDIOT FAMILY AT HOME

Written by A J Stairmand

Illustrated by Teeny Barnett

Published by Stairmand Publishing 2012

A CIP catalogue record for this book is available from the British Library

ISBN 978-0-9569234-3-1

Prepared and printed by

York Publishing Services
64 Hallfield Road
Layerthorpe
York YO31 7ZQ

www.yps-publishing.co.uk

BIOGRAPHY

Anne Stairmand was born in North Yorkshire, living much of her life in villages near the Cleveland Hills. After graduating, she worked in education, teaching in both primary and secondary schools in the south east, working in the advisory service and as part of a leadership team.

Dividing her time, she now writes books for children and adults, and has her own business as a bespoke jeweller, with her own hallmark and stamp, specialising in silver, pearls and commissions. She is married with a grown up family and lives on the Suffolk Essex border.

CHAPTER ONE

C an you imagine being called an Idiot – or worse still, having it as a surname, the bit after your real name? Can you imagine having to use the word Idiot all the time as part of your everyday life? Luckily, most of the population have surnames such as Smith, Jones, Harper, Stones, Clarke, Carter and Fields, so it's nice and easy and, far more importantly, not something to be teased about by people. As we know, having a stupid name means being punished mercilessly – unless you are the child of a rock star, movie star, celebrity or a footballer. Though, tragically, most footballers' children's first names are the problem! Not least because they are quite often named after a fruit, vegetable, colour, drink, shoe, tube station, airport, hotel, chewing gum or aftershave. So for this particular group of children, we really need to have universal sympathy for their uneducated and unprofessional parents who will pay truckloads of money for their beautiful, sweet, articulate offspring to become brain surgeons and judges.

Let's get back to the focus of the story. I am going to introduce you to a family of Idiots and, for what it's worth, they truly suit their surname. So you and I can sit back with our crisps, chocolate or apples and enjoy discovering what happens in the Idiots' daily life.

Again, if you have a dad called Mr Jones, the chances are he probably wears a suit, leaves the house at eight o'clock every morning, cleans his car on a Saturday and never over-spends on his credit card. He will always take you ten-pin bowling, clear the crisp packets out of your sports bag, make you eat salad and always, always, always make you brush your teeth. So, as a child, you can't go wrong – so even though he will never take you to a hippy concert, let you stay up all night or give you the loan of his car, you know he is looking after you and his love is constant. To be honest, this is probably the same for most fathers, except the surnames vary, not to mention their weight, height, lack of hair, the range of dreadful shirts and ties they wear and, most importantly, the amount of money you can squeeze from them.

Mr Idiot's grandfather, Tuttersmat, had escaped from the lands of Siberia on the back of a Russian milk float, which carried goats instead of bottles. After months of drinking goats' milk, growing a beard and picking up several sentences in goat, he became goat-like and became the advisor to the chief goat – quite an honour. Of course, pounding across the Siberian landscape was cold, bitterly cold in fact; it was somewhere into big minuses which meant Tuttersmat had to snuggle into the goats' woolly coats. He was lucky as they didn't charge him for the loan of the warmth of their coats; he on the other hand, took no notice when they passed wind near his face.

On reaching the shores of Europe, Tuttersmat and the Russian milk float went their separate ways, all promising in goat language to keep in contact, but all knowing this was the end, and life would now be very different. To cut a long story short, Tuttersmat ended up in Hull, met the future Mrs Idiot and began the very first school of goat language for adults. Although it was unique and frequently visited by government officials, who appeared in white coats to have close conversations with the Idiots (who always had to wear strange contraptions which tied their hands behind their backs), they became famous for the goat school.

However, as you know, if you are learning another language, goats, like humans, have different dialects. So the harsh Russian twang at the end of every bleat had to be adapted to suit the needs of West Yorkshire's shamelessly unruly goats. Cutting the story even shorter, Tuttersmat was recognised for his work with goats; awarded the Golden Milk Bottle from the Queen's Dairy, an unquestionable honour, and found his fame in the Guinness Book of Records – or the equivalent about then. With fame came money, popularity, more money and, of course, more goats.

The Idiots, like all new money, built a monstrosity of a castle with goat-shaped windows and held brash parties where everyone was swathed in goats' milk and champagne – obviously not at the same time. Mrs Idiot had her favourite chosen goats which became nannies to her four goat-loving children. Of course, having spent zillions of tasteless money on something that resembled a hybrid between a stately home and a goat shed, the Idiots were the equivalent of the footballers today!

They took their goats to parliament, declaring the rights of the woolly pack to keep their hair, or to have a percentage of the money made on their coats. When Tuttersmat died, sheep, goats and other four-legged creatures were in mourning. And, of course, his coffin resembled a goat.

Splutterap Idiot was the eldest son of the Idiot dynasty and was keen to make his own mark and reputation in the business world, so he decided to expand the goat school to include a new and rare beast, the kangaroo. Obviously, not having the internet caused communication problems and Splutterap, not being particularly bright, had to trek across the world, by foot, train, camel and boat, to get to Australia, where the country was packed to the brim with convicts wearing very sharp stripy overalls. Splutterap, as the name suggested, had the tragic disability of spluttering, with saliva dribbling from his mouth when he talked. Whilst he was the eldest of the Idiots, he truly was the most foolish and moronic out of the children. For example, in order to get on well with the convicts, he offered those soon to be free a place to stay in his stately home back in England. He bought extra food and wine for his chosen convicts and bought five of the local prisons as an investment.

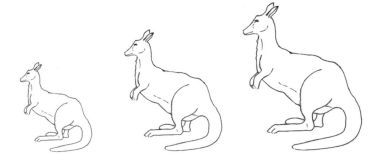

When hunting for kangaroos, he got lost in the bush and was befriended by a herd of buffalo that spent much of the time using him as a multi-coloured football. However, once he was over the initial breakage of bones, constant bruising and biting, Splutterap decided buffalo were the new goat: now this could have been to do with the furry coat, the bandy legs, the big snout, or the dribbling mouth. Perhaps you are thinking the new Idiot of the dynasty had met creatures of his own kind: they looked alike, had similar mannerisms and both needed a good brushing. Splutterap, an ardent follower of his father, made the decision to introduce the language of buffalo to the great British public.

True to his name, Mr Idiot gave each buffalo his own ticket and carriage on the train in Melbourne for the north coast. Many passengers, intrigued and horrified by the new type of traveller, tried to complain about the behaviour of the animals, only to find that Splutterap Idiot had bought the train company and was in the process of designing buffalo suites. Of course, the banality of the situation made him famous once again, just like his father, and soon, wherever Splutterap and the buffalo went, thousands of adoring fans followed. People sold their houses to give money to his cause. They cried when they managed to touch his hands.

Such was his absurd fame that, by the time they arrived at Portsmouth, the King greeted him with the Changing of the Guard and a fanfare only suitable for a royal marriage or death. Even though he was balding, fat and greasy with terrible blackheads on his nose, face and in his ears, in dreadful need of a bath, a shave and new teeth, Splutterap was surrounded by the most beautiful women in the land. It was at the quayside in Portsmouth where he met the future Mrs Idiot. Blonde, beautiful, she chewed grass and spoke in words of a single syllable often intonated with 'ooohs' and 'arhhhhs'.

So, the present head of the Idiot dynasty was born fourteen months after their wedding, where goats and buffalo intermingled with aristocracy and leading figures of the day. Piggersnaff Idiot was a gentle child who, like previous Idiots, played, worked and talked to goats and buffalo. Strangely enough, although he had the biggest country estate for miles around, plus the best ice cream and games, he wasn't very popular with other children at school. This could have been because when he was unhappy or angry with others at school, he sent in the goats or buffalo to sort them out.

Piggersnaff was an only child, so the pressure to outdo previous heads of the dynasty was very important. He too had to be a true Idiot and make a name for himself, get a royal award and go in the Guinness Book of Records – which had now been written. As he grew up he much preferred the fast moving life in London and asked his father if he could have a castle near Chelsea's football ground. He demanded that his devoted father buy a few buildings then knock them down so he could have a modern day castle – not some elegant, tasteful place representing history – but some modern, glitzy, rather trashy extravaganza. Much to his delight, Old Man Idiot, now doddering about with his goats, was only too pleased to keep his fat, young, greasy-haired, brown-toothed hapless teenager happy. So he contacted government officials (plus the Queen and the Duke of Westminster) and knocked down the ghastly historic monuments and buildings running from the Strand to the river bank of the Thames.

9

Of course there was human outcry; even the Duke was rather rattled at losing some of the buildings. But you know what? Money talks and boy did it. Old Man Idiot, as Piggersnaff called him, had accumulated all the prisons in Europe and made prisoners and their families pay to lock up their thieves, convicts and murderers. The Old Man's wealth was seriously massive. When Splutterap had made his first coup buying prisons in Australia, little did he think that making them a paying concern would make him so rich. Being the true Idiot that he was, each prison sponsored his goats and buffalo and all inmates had to have language lessons in goat and buffalo – a dying, but unique art.

So there you have it, a potted history of the now famous Idiot dynasty where Idiots moved with some of the most powerful people in the land and around the world. Of course the new castle near Chelsea football ground was gross, vulgar, and full of gold taps, loos and sinks. Even the dish cloths had fine strands of twenty-two carat gold woven into the material – making each wash a golden experience – and Piggersnaff was 'almost' happy.

Piggersnaff Idiot married Jimmelta Chew Van De Bratt, the third daughter of a German tycoon who had invented the first talking tables and chairs for lonely people. His empire stretched across the whole universe, as each table (very cleverly, may I say), had a series of topics, different voices and background music to keep customers happy. The only downside happened to be in restaurants, where the blur of conversations resonated to levels similar to that of a riot or a football match. Nevertheless, the Chew Van De Bratts, who also had strange and most unlikely beginnings – which I won't bore you with at the moment – were disgustingly rich and, like the Idiots, abhorred the very thought of taste, style or elegance.

So here we are in the home of Mr and Mrs Idiot, in central London near Chelsea's football ground. Piggersnaff decided to stay in Bullion Castle after the marriage to the divine and most delectable Jimmelta. Luckily for the rest of the nation, Piggers and Jimmi were well suited and spent most of the day herding goats with golden necklaces from one room to the other. I suppose you want me to describe the place they and their offspring live in, so you have a picture.

From the Thames, towering above the roofline and in gold, is the outline of a spire in the shape of a goat, the family mast, a herald which looms ready to pounce. Leading up to the enormous wrought iron gates, which are speckled with shapes of goats, are two cameras. One to see who the visitors are, the other plugged into the football ground so the family can always spot what's going on. Old Man Idiot was very proud of the deal: this castle and all the gold from South Africa had been expensive – he'd had to sell three of his Australian prisons to riase the money immediately. All the prisoners were given dinghies and shipped out to the middle of the Atlantic and any who made the journey home would be offered a job cleaning the gold in Bullion Castle. Sadly, only a few survived.

Once inside the grand drive leading up to the entrance, an avenue of sandstone animal statues in different coloured finishes guided the visitor to the wide, brightly coloured steps, each one making a musical note as part of a song. Once the pear-shaped golden bell was rung, a butler dressed in pink and green appeared immediately out of nowhere and ushered you into the hall.

Then you heard the screams and laughter of the little Idiots from the rooms nearby, accompanied by a yell of anger, obviously from their mother. As you can imagine, Jimmelta, who was used to being the centre of attention, was determined that the names of her divine offspring would be unusual, thought-

13

provoking and different from all those pathetic footballers' names. Being a woman of great depth and one who took issues in life quite seriously, she was torn between naming the children after charities, or the environment. After much thought, she cancelled both and decided to follow her heart, so all the names were after styles of material, her first love.

Tall and stout with a wave of ginger hair, the eldest son also had a fondness for doughnuts, though he didn't eat as many as Jimmelta. Gingham Idiot was already full of surprises; he spent most of his time climbing anything that resembled a mountain and insisted that he slept in a bubble tent on the roof of the castle along with the odd goat or buffalo. Jimmelta thought he had an adorable personality, always smiling and never demanding too much, and he loved pasta, morning noon and night.

Very much the tomboy, always wearing jeans, the second child had long, curly, golden-red hair that was always stuffed under a baseball cap. Polka was eight and a half and collected squirrels, much to the admiration of Old Man Idiot and Piggersnaff. So far, the collection had taken over most of the attic floor in the castle and, true to form, she had a tree planted in the castle so that they felt comfortable. Of course she was in her second year of squirreling and was able to talk and squeak and had thought of expanding the banal family tradition, though her greatest claim to fame was being able to drink Coke through a snorkel. Jimmelta did despair of Polka, who had the potential to be such a cute girl, but insisted on wearing flippers with any clothes, which ruled her out of being introduced into society.

Paisley was six and screamed all the time, demanded ice cream and toffee noodles at each meal, and as a result had rotting teeth, spotty skin and a bursting waist line. For some reason he didn't collect animals, wish to climb mountains, want to dive or even want to own a spaceship. Both parents were worried: a lack of ambition or eccentricity wasn't something either was accustomed to. It was certainly a worry for the grandparents.

Then there was Kidston who was just, well... ordinary. Small, tubby, with bright blue eyes and a shock of black curly hair, he spent most of his day discovering new places to hide and disturbing the servants. However, he was very popular with the Inherited Australian Convicts who often gave him piggy backs while they were doing their countless chores. At two or three years old (Jimmelta couldn't quite remember), he played on his tricycle, didn't speak to goats and wanted to live in a high rise flat in Bethnal Green or Corby – wherever that was.

So there we have it, a family of Idiots who had the opportunity to make and shape the world just like their ancestors with everything to encourage a vision for the future – from an Idiot's point of view of course!

CHAPTER TWO

'Piggers, what are you doing today my sweet thing?' trilled the guzzling Jimmelta between mouthfuls of doughnuts.

'Buying, my sweet delicious Doughy, just buying,' he replied, sipping from his golden cup containing the rarest black Chinese tea from Harrods, 'and you know how I like to do that.' This was said with typical Idiot firmness implying a successful day ahead. His long, pointed nose beaked into the paper, leaving only a vision of curly black hair, which nodded as he read different articles. Thin, dangling fingers with wide nails grabbed the edges of each sheet with a great intensity as the information was digested. When he peered over the top of it to respond to his hungry wife, you were met by black green eyes shrouded by thick, heavy rimmed glasses, which dominated his spotty and greasy skin. This, dear reader, wasn't the best image to start the day.

'Well what are you buying?' responded his other half, spooning the sugar from the bottom of her golden cup with her fingers and licking them.

'Bolivia,' Piggersnaff defiantly said, browsing down the shares from the IG (Idiots' Guide).

'Oh, I thought that was a drink,' said Jimmelta.

'No darling, sweet Doughy that you are, of course, mistaking Bolivia for Bournville, never mind…'

'Oh Piggers I thought Bournville was a town…'

'No, darling! No! BourneMOUTH is a town. Bournville is the stuff we drink before bed and Bolivia is a small country in South America.' His patience with "his" most beautiful Jimmelta was in the process of snapping.

'It's hard to imagine that a little letter at the beginning of the alphabet could cause so much confusion. I DREAD TO THINK WHAT THE Ys and Zs do! Hard to imagine a "B" having such power… and darling, thank you for the detailed replies. Now I know why I married you. Would I like this little place, you know the one starting with a "B"? Could I pop over and snap up a few things?' she asked, leaning back on her golden armchair and yawning.

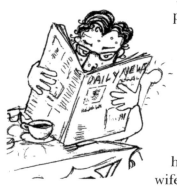

Piggers glanced up from the paper, his eyes filled with horror at such a simplistic view on life.

'Jimmelta, speak up or use the phone by your place! I can't hear you. Use the phone.' Pigger's mouth twitched, he couldn't understand his wife's simple view on life and was glad she had no intentions of doing anything worthwhile in society. The thought made him shudder. Her stupidity might just cause an international incident!

Obediently she picked up the receiver of the jade hand-carved phone on the golden table and continued her conversation. 'Do you think you could get some more palladium? I really need it for some bits and pieces.'

'Can't you just take a bit off the chair and solder it into some jewels? I can't just keep buying the world's resources because you need one or two things… darling this is serious stuff.' Piggersnaff had shared his work countless times but it all came down to two things – money and happiness – with Jimmelta.

'I know, I know.' She scanned around the dining hall where the servants were skating in with the next course of pancakes soaked in maple syrup and the sweetest mango juice, freshly pulped. She frowned at the length of the golden table, the golden chairs, golden knives and forks and, of course, golden plates. How she wished for lovely Cath Kidston tablecloths, cups and saucers with little flowers painted on the sides and plastic knives in pink, blue and orange; this bachelor furniture really had to go, but now wasn't the time to argue.

'I was thinking about getting a tablecloth made for this,' she said, pointing, 'then I thought it might be nice to have some new plates and cups and stuff...'

'Jimmelta! I've had this golden table since I was a teenager. Old Man Idiot bought Saudi so I could have the chairs made, the stuff you don't like is better than Dotty's next door AND... Last time Dotty had a state banquet she sent one of her servants to borrow our stuff! Doesn't it say something when the heads of NATO used our plates? I got twelve requests for the design in gold... Jimmelta, haven't you got *ANY TASTE?* I'm off on my shuttle!' With that he stormed on to his buggy and made his way down to the entrance hall where he was carried by buffalo to his own personal shuttle – gold of course.

I think you have an idea how the Idiot family live – appalling opulence, something unbeknown to man. Even the tycoons and zillionaires had to give respect where it was due, as nobody had seen Piggersnaff Idiot complete one day's work in his life – yet his place on the rich list was exclusive. Still, let's get back to this repugnant family and look in on how the parents managed their offspring.

Just as the shuttle was about to take off, Piggers got a phone call. 'For you sir. I'm afraid it's your beautiful and intelligent wife... obviously missing you,' sneered a small, long-nosed man with greasy black hair, garlic breath, black cavity-ridden teeth and a boil on his cheek. Grabbing the phone he barked, 'Wha' d'you want now, Brazil?'

'No! I forgot to tell you that Big Skule rang about Gingham in class – I spoke to the head, Precarious Pinchingthorpe-Munching-Mop-Phillips, such a man. You know the one I mean: very short. Ties that glisten and grab students! THE ONE WITH THE TIES THAT SLITHER AROUND CORNERS LOOKING FOR DANGEROUS KIDS! You know, when he smiles his jaw crackles.' This was hard work getting Piggers to remember who the head was, possibly because he'd never had anything to do with the school – except for writing the cheques.

So she continued, 'Gingham is hell bent on writing, obviously they're concerned and don't want to cause a fuss, but I think it's getting quite serious. Apparently he asked for a dictionary, yes I know. Then to make matters worse, he wrote a paragraph with something called… er… complex sentences. I thought they were slimming powders. Piggers are you listening? This is serious stuff. We need to talk to him and go through his report card. I suppose as long as he doesn't get into this writing habit we should be alright. I spoke to Dotty, she said all her four went through the writing phase and are fine now; the eldest is hoping to be King and really turned things around. Dotty was saying that once he got it out of his system he went back to normal things like buying counties and being head of the church…'

Piggers had had enough. He'd have a word with Gingham, have a man-to-man talk and get to the heart of the problem. He pondered on the difficulties of growing up in a brilliant family. The stress and expectation might be too much; perhaps Gingham needed his own island. After all, he was ten. Ah what it was to be an Idiot!

Polka arrived at breakfast with great speed on her skates and loudly announced that she wanted to live in a caravan when she grew up, as life in Bullion Castle was boring.

'I want to have my breakfast off a stove and have mouldy toast which is burnt, an' I want to have a sleeping bag – they look fun.' Glancing around the dining hall she scowled as her curly hair covered her blue eyes. Picking up the phone by her seat, Polka informed her mother that she was going on strike.

'Darling, what's the point of going on strike when there's nothing to complain about? It just seems so *silly*,' replied Jimmelta, who found it hard to comprehend the stupidity of the statement.

'Well that's just it, I am eight and haven't had a rebellion yet, everybody has to grow up and I am bored. Anyway, can't we have some plastic knives an' stuff, I hate this gold! It's so boring. Everything except school is BORING!' With that, she slammed her golden spoon down on the golden table and threw the golden cup of chocolate on the gold-leafed floor.

'Darling, don't do that. I will have to get one of the Inherited Australian Convicts to clear it up again, and they are already cleaning the gold guttering. Why would you want plastic cutlery? You can't have everything you want. After all, money doesn't grow on trees!' Jimmelta had snapped. A husband who wouldn't let her have a Cath Kidston tablecloth, a son who wanted to write and now, a spoilt daughter who wanted plastic knives and forks! She really needed to have break, perhaps Piggers could buy her a little pad, and she'd heard St Kitts was up for grabs. Family life could be so stressful.

Finishing her mound of doughnuts, Jimmelta skimmed through the list of clothes given to her by the servants on duty, and scanning the list she noted with horror that her daughter was wearing socks from... a department store!

All the clothes in the house, including socks and such like were, naturally, couture; the best animals slaughtered, silk spun and cashmere woven from Siberian woolly backs. Lagerfeld, or rather Karl, would be so sad and disappointed in her family. Such shame, no wonder she needed therapy, children should never be seen, heard or EVER be allowed to think. And it was only seven o'clock. In Jimmelta's book, it was more like midnight. This unearthly, cruel, evil time of the day was meant to be for poor people scratching something out of erm, erm, a dustbin? In future, she decided, the children and the family would be presented to her one by one, a list of clothes in hand, at a more reasonable time.

Yelling at one of the Inherited Australian Convicts, she demanded freshly ground coffee from Brazil immediately. The old, blind, toothless man bowed and shuffled away, pulling his left, lame leg after him.

'Can't you walk properly yet?' bawled Jimmelta, in a foul mood now as she watched Polka standing on the table pulling at the golden chandeliers. The servant muttered something under his breath and Jimmelta roared, 'Why don't you speak English? The buffalo make more sense than you!'

'Mummy, can we have some new Inherited Australian Convicts? I could have one of my own and then feed him to the buffalo, just like Grandpa Chew Van De Bratt did with...'

'Enough! Get on your shuttle and fly to school. Where are Paisley and Gingham? Polka, phone the servants to find them now! I WANT ANOTHER DOUGHNUT NOW!'

As we know, a bad-tempered mother at the start of the week with three children to go is not a good sign. However, there are small mercies to be had. The rude, aggressive and downright ignorant behaviour displayed by a thoroughly disgustingly stupid woman who, without realising it, aptly lives up to her name, and will be, as they say, hoist on her own petard.

CHAPTER THREE

'**B**ig Skule' was the envy of every child in the country, as the curriculum, the only one nationwide, was based on the each student's personal choices of how they liked to spend their day. It was run by the infamous Precarious Pinchingthorpe-Munching-Mop-Phillips who was either revered or reviled by parents across the land. A little man, both in stature and of course, in principle, his life focused on fame and MONEY. Dear reader let me tell you just the tiniest bit about him and how after life's struggles, he came to preside over the future of the most affluent, socially insignificant students the nation had to offer. Then you can understand…

As a child, Precarious Pinchingthorpe-Munching–Mop-Phillips had been adored by his mother, abhorred by his classmates, ignored by his teachers, was bored with school and was deplored by most people he came to know. In fact, there were so many "oreds" that by the time he was five, and having been abandoned in the sand pit by other children, he wore magnificent bow ties in spectacular colours to make an impression. By the age of ten he had developed the ability to weave his way into the confidences of friends and foes, using information as a blackmail tool to further his career. By thirteen the bow ties were replaced by handmade ties of dazzling colours and exquisite fabrics woven by Tibetan monkeys and Siberian goats. The masterpieces were indeed the hallmark that would help him to succeed in future life. By seventeen, after an explosive introduction to the world of politics where he was the only candidate for his local seat in Knutismore, after many egg hurling episodes over his manifesto, he decided his duty was to guide the younger nation.

Actually, he thought that given the splendid skills of deception, obsequious greed, a thirst for power and a deep hatred of being so small, he decided to run a school. So after finishing an education as an undercover agent, he decided to open one, make it private and cash in on stupid parents with loads of spare money.

Big Skule allowed him to be master of all, be in charge of a vision and nod, with a snivelling smug smile, to the richest, the most foolish, most tasteless parents and their offspring. So that's how the three elder Idiots came to be in this establishment. Jimmelta had seen it advertised. Like all parents dreaming of the best education, and since Jimmelta still hadn't worked out all the letters of the alphabet and only stuck to the ones she liked, Big Skule seemed to be her idea of perfection. So this was how Gingham spent his day speaking goat, learning how to glide, and developing intense skills in strange subjects such as bat collecting. The school was under strict instructions by all parents that writing was forbidden, working with numbers above a hundred was completely out of order, dictionaries were a definite no and exploring gravity should only relate to getting food from your plate into your mouth.

As you can imagine, this place really was every child's dream. Then to top it all, each student had their own personal teacher who they liked to "hang out" with. Depending on how the students felt when they arrived at Skule, reflected on how each one spent their day. When the rest of the country read about this new educational establishment, there was an outcry from everyone – even the Prime Minister, who slated Precarious Pinchingthorpe-Munching-Mop-Phillip's brazen desire to de-educate the richest youth in society. This was followed by an outcry from parents horrified at the standards – or lack of them. And, of course, there was a revolution from students up and down the land, demanding that the PM2 curriculum abandon the need for textbooks, pens and exams.

WORN BY HEADTEACHER

Jimmelta had a soft spot for Precarious Pinchingthorpe-Munching-Mop-Phillips after he had worn her diamond platform shoes to a parents' evening and introduced her as the most supportive and exciting parent whose life was genuinely golden.

'Fellow parents, adorable students, splendid governors and of course, my most revered colleagues...' he slithered a knowing smile around the hall, brimming with expectantly haplessly proud parents. 'I know, as we gather yet again to celebrate the genius of our younger generation, may I...' he gestured opening his arms out to the crowd, checking his tie in a mirror tucked in the palm of his hand, 'praise your good work, the good work of our devoted colleagues and... my utter brilliance!' To which there was an outburst of clapping and cheering.

Dear reader, it was easy to see why students wished to go to school each day, why teachers didn't need to teach and why PM2 was quite simply... rolling in it. The money flowed like water and he smiled as he was clocking up the thousands of pounds from each parent. Being a "Child Innovator", not a head teacher, strengthened his plans to wreak his revenge for those bitter memories of his own childhood and unhappy youth. We will, of course, come back to the machiavellian leader later on, but let's for now get back to Bullion Castle.

CHAPTER FOUR

One of the greatest things about being average or less than average is the average expectation others may have of you. This is enormous comfort and I am sure there were times when the Idiots' only dream was to be normal, average; to have baked beans on a chipped white plate; to argue about which programme to watch on TV; to have a supermarket tee shirt, and to eat takeaways and do the Lottery. Gingham wanted to write and use paragraphs; he wanted to "make something of himself". Polka's dream was simple: plastic knives and forks and a sleeping bag, such pleasing tastes.

By the time breakfast had finished, three servants had been sacked and one had been fed to the buffalo for a snack. Jimmelta insisted that the freshly ground coffee straight from Brazil wasn't a wish, it was a necessity, and the green eco thing really was 'quite a bore'. Paisley only wanted toffee noodles and immediately threw his skates at some of the Inherited Australian Convicts who were already polishing the table at the far end of the hall. It would only take them four days working shifts to finish it.

Leaving the children to scream and be dragged to school, Jimmelta decided to rest her huge body on one of the sofas Piggersnaff had designed for her. He loved her dearly, and nothing was too much; he had several incredibly large sofas built for her lard-like frame. How she hated Monday mornings when Piggers was away. The children, she decided, were difficult and her life, she decided, was terribly cruel and harsh, and she didn't know what was to become of her. To top it all, she had to get some more Inherited Australian Convicts from the agency: more money.

Well readers, I bet you're glad you don't live in Bullion Castle, have a dangerously fat mother, eat off golden tables and worse, cannot write. So just before you moan, remember it takes an Idiot not to appreciate the importance of education.

Only an Idiot would encourage goat and buffalo talking, only an Idiot would name their children after styles and types of material.

Only a group of Idiots would act like this.
And remember: this was just breakfast!

CHAPTER FIVE

Nobody loves a birthday like an Idiot and, true to form, the requests from all the family were strange, if not a bit weird. You and I might wish for a new bike, shoes or a football kit, a day out at a theme park, maybe a slap-up meal in a fast food place; we would be content with any of the above, plus a little money.

Not so in the Idiot family. Piggersnaff, used to being spoilt as a child, thought it only right that his offspring had the same. The first birthday on the calendar was Polka's; at seven she had requested to have her own mountains. Piggers naturally bought her a third of the Scottish Highlands, promising her the rest when there was a change of government. Two years on, approaching her birthday, Jimmelta asked Polka what she would like.

'Darling, now that you are eight going on nine, what would you like? I thought a little party with a thousand of your closest friends would be rather nice...' Her voice trailed off as she saw her daughter skating down the corridors of Bullion Castle, hacking the servants with her squirrels, chasing the fittest to the stairs at the end.

'Nope, I don't want a party. Everyone has them – they're BORING... I WANT... I WANT... I WANT...' deep in thought, Polka circled the few remaining Inherited Australian Convicts, sticking out her tongue in a defiant manner. 'I want... Paris.'

'Paris darling, oh you mean Hilton, umm isn't she a little old for you?' twittered Jimmelta, trying on the new diamond shoes handmade from the mines in Africa.

'No I mean Paris,' retorted Polka.

'Well if perfume's all you want that's fine.'

'NO! Paris the city! I want my own city, just like you have your own island! STUPID MUMMY!' With that, our delightful little girl stormed off, throwing a golden chair at any remaining servants who were now dressed in riot gear. Experience had taught them over the years that when any Idiot was angry, you were never to trust their judgement and should think only of your safety.

After much argument, Jimmelta managed to persuade her daughter that buying a whole city had many drawbacks, mainly litter on the streets, dog poo in parks and tramps, who would expect Polka to give them handouts.

'Really darling, buying a city is more trouble than it's worth, what with all the pollution, European laws, and…' she added quietly, 'those people who don't wash and have smelly underwear. Darling you'd have to give out panty parcels, just like food parcels in the war. And you know, only the rich ones wash! The money you would have to pay out for body deodorant for French men would be bigger than my national food bill for Latvia. It's just not worth it. Let me buy you a football team or something small and quaint…' Jimmelta trilled on between mouthfuls of doughnuts, whilst Polka nibbled on the nail clippings of some of the Inherited Australian Convicts, marinated in peach and toffee cream, a new Idiot delight.

'Mummy, because I think we have quite a bit of money and some people might think I am spoilt… I am going to start a charity for children who…' she added thoughtfully, 'have been forced to write.'

'OH POLKA! How incredibly clever of you darling! The struggle some of these children have in camps – just like the war…'

'Mummy! You idiot! That's school!' interrupted Polka. 'I'm talking about a nation forcefed on writing…sentences…'

'Darling, I have a better idea. Why don't you go into politics? We need your sort of innovation to move this country forward! Of course, you can't wear your flippers in the House of Loot... it wouldn't do...'

Jimmelta was already imagining her next garden party with Dotty's son a King, and her daughter, leader of the House of Loot. Only an Idiot lives in their own mess, convinced that the idea of self improvement is a joke. We now have the fear of real Idiots in politics who think that delaying and curbing academic achievements is going to take our country to greater places. Polka had a vision of crayons, whilst her mother on the other hand, thought that Polka was just the material to support

young people in difficult circumstances, force-fed to write in rows in classrooms, with that dreadful thing called... homework. Yes, she thought, as she examined her increasingly blotchy waistline, the elitist system could suit everyone. After all, this was the twenty-first century; slavery should be abolished – well, except for the Inherited Australian Convicts.

Polka phoned her thousand closest friends; this took the best part of a week and she told them about the sleepover and the use of Dotty's pad up at the Mall for extra space. Dotty, being a most reasonable queen, and quite tolerant of new money, said, after keep fit, it would be fine for Polka to stay with her friends but they had to leave the Inherited Australian Convicts at home – bad publicity.

So in the Idiot household there was much excitement. At nine, Polka had taken the noble decision to go into politics and now she had to form a party, have a manifesto and give it a name. This, dear reader, is how The Eraser Party was formed. Gingham decided to be in charge of the money and was aptly called Money Bags. Teabags Pixie Spoon, daughter of the world's greatest plate spinner, was to be in charge of Foreign Eclairs and Affairs, while Chubby Van Der Swot was in charge of investments. Masky Cara Snitter Du Pew was to lead the party on the De-Education Bill ensuring that all students had the right to a de-education, allowing them to pursue the trivial things in life so they were prepared for a life of opulence and luxury. Paisley also had a role; to check the constant supply of toffee cream snacks.

How proud the Idiots were of Polka. Jimmelta simply couldn't wait for the next local coffee morning at the Church of Harvey Nichols to tell the other mummies about the birthday event. She mused as she went into her gold wardrobe picking out Egyptian stones from her latest pyramid, to go with her rabbit spun tracksuit. How fortuitous that she had such bright, clever, marvellous children who wished to

be pioneers for the next generation. As she eyed up her new stones stuck on her forehead, she looked at the twenty-four carat gold wardrobe and wished, for the millionth time, that she could have a Marks and Spencer closet, lined with Cath Kidston scented paper. Her life really wasn't fair and Piggers was just so boring. Everybody had Cath Kidston things, why couldn't she? Was she asking for the earth? No, she already had most of that, so why couldn't she have something new and Cath Kidston-y?

CHAPTER SIX

Well, we will leave everyone to get on with the preparations for the party for Polka, but let's just check on Gingham, the eldest Idiot, already planning his birthday one month away.

'So what do you wish to do for your big day?' bellowed Piggersnaff to Gingham, who was messing about with the gold tables, chipping bits off and flicking them across the dining hall.

'I don't want anything posh like Polka. I want to go on the tube,' said Gingham quietly as he knew his father didn't like the tube.

'Isn't that one of these programmes on television?' retorted his father, wiping his greasy face on a towel from the excessively unhealthy diet of fried eggs and sausages. Gingham, looking disgustedly at the mounds of eggs smothered in the most extra fine olive oil, decided he wasn't having a repeat performance of Polka's conversation and cut it short.

'Look, I don't want a million friends over for tea, or a party: I want to travel on the tube – you know, from Bank to Covent Garden and change to Oxford Street.'

'Idiots don't do the tube,' responded his father firmly but quietly. 'No son or child of mine needs to go on the tube.'

'That's what I want AND I'm going to do it! You don't even have to buy it!' shouted Gingham, kicking the golden table with his silver plated and palladium roller skates.

'Stop interrupting when I AM TALKING!' bawled Piggersnaff at the top of his voice, rattling the windows of the long hall and loosening the teeth of the oldest servants clinging on to the curtain rails for dear life. They hated it when Piggers got angry, but even more when the children also yelled – the noise was like a jumbo jet leaving the garden, a shuttle going into orbit, or a hurricane descending on Bullion Castle. All the Inherited Australian Convicts agreed that a stint in prison was better than a run-in with any Idiot.

Well, how right they were. Who wants to see greasy, fat, spot-exploding people having such tantrums close up? I don't, do you? As you know, people like this spoilt, repugnant, deplorable family only ever think of themselves – even if they are destined to be thick and stupid all their lives.

And another thing dear reader. You must be asking, just like me, how come people this STUPID have so much money and incredible wealth?

And why are they not doing something worthwhile with it like helping others? It is hard to imagine a more socially unsuitable family to be the bastions of taste and sophistication, but there you have it!

Let's get back to this episode about Gingham demanding a "normal birthday", you know, a little independence and bucketloads of normality. All he wanted were his three favourite friends, who happened to be the cleverest boys in Big Skule.

'Piggers, no son of mine is going on a *TUBE*,' yelled Jimmelta from the top of the golden stairs to her long suffering husband who was preening his stout, portly frame in the mirror whilst one of the Inherited Australian Convicts brushed his greasy, egg-fried hair, another handing him tea in a golden cup, whilst finally one of the older convicts tried, with difficulty, to read the IDIOT Stock Market Guide.

'Look Doughy, I know that there will be people on them and of course, they won't be dressed in Gabbana, Dior or normal clothes, but come on, the boy needs a little adventure...' twittered Piggers, wafting his tea away so he could pick a spot on the end of his nose.

'They SMELL! You know that! Those... THOSE... PEOPLE!' Jimmelta screamed from the top of the golden stairs, shouting with such rage that the spit from her saliva cascaded down the golden hand rails to the floor, landing in a syrupy, bubblised pulp. 'NO! NO! NO! What about the dirt and the germs? Gingham isn't used to people with common colds, his have always been exclusive!' Jimmelta stamped her foot, snapping her emerald heel. Of course, we, the readers, have to snigger at such a disgusting statement, as there could not have been more disgraceful and unhygienic behaviour from the fashion-conscious Right Honourable Mrs Idiot.

'Well, you talk to him then,' replied Piggers, flicking one of the Inherited Australian Convicts, who had been begging for the crumbs of his cake off the lapel of his most expensive coat. 'I'm off to buy something.'

'Why don't you stay at home like other husbands and help to sort out the problem?' screamed his wife hysterically. 'Why are you always buying? Why can't I have a Cath Kidston tablecloth? Everybody else has one?' She crumpled into a heap on the stairs and rather resembled a packet of doughnuts squashed and broken and cried, loudly. The servants all put in their ear plugs.

Out of the whole ramshackle family, Jimmelta had the worst cry, worst trill, worst stamp, worst snort, worst flounce, but worst of all... she really had not only the worst manners, she had the worst ankles and arm pits, which were flabby and smelt of doughnuts.

The Inherited Australian Convicts knew the rest of the week was going to be horrid, and, like all good survivors of the war, they made a plan of attack to support Gingham. Down below in the servants' quarters, the conversations displayed general support for Gingham and an outright repulsion for Jimmelta, Piggersnaff and Paisley because they were also fat, greasy and incredibly rude. They also knew that if THE FAT DOUGHY, as they called her, wanted something, she always got it. This meant that poor old Gingham would end up having a horrible, rich, overly-spoilt birthday party.

CHAPTER SEVEN

So here once again we have it, the tastelessness of wealth, where a child is not allowed to have a birthday on the cheap. It has to be the biggest, the boldest, the most trivial and, of course, the most expensive. Indeed it must be at this time, that you, the readers, are just so grateful for your parents, your simple ordinary lives and the knowledge that the like of Jimmelta is always somebody else's mother – and not yours. Such simple and truly fantastic blessings are yours.

The battle of the tubes lasted roughly a week. As a punishment for having absolutely no taste, Gingham was made to watch reality television cleaning shows and then complete a questionnaire on them. The programmes lasted an hour each, with the contestants being holed up in something like a land tip. The winner generally was the one who hadn't died from a disease or lost a limb due to gangrene. Jimmelta wanted to show her son the true horrors of living on the other side, outside Bullion Castle. Remembering the problems Dotty had with her sons when they wanted to give their palaces to the poor and eat sandwiches from a local supermarket, she phoned and asked for some advice, only to be told that there was a state banquet in the evening and Dotty had gone for a facial.

Gingham was excited. His first visit on the underground was going to be amazing. He couldn't wait to collect his ticket and stand in a queue with other people. This, dear reader, was where his parents were so stupid and so aptly named. Intelligent people, wealthy people, normal people, would have encouraged their children to have a perfectly normal existence, shopping in Tesco's, going to the cinema and enjoying the fun of the city. Actually, to you and me, the birthday experience was a bit of a non event, but to Gingham Idiot it was stupendous; except for the part where the public had to wash their hands and wear gloves at the entrance of each tube. The Inherited Australian Convicts were dropped into the mouths of stations, spraying a new germ-killing deodorant designed for persistently, perspiring, putrid, spot-bearing stenches that clung to even the cleanest and the most hygienic individuals. 'At least,' thought Piggersnaff, 'this should keep "her" happy.'

Oh, if only that was true! Jimmelta, after weeks of tantrums, accepted that Gingham had to grow up and lead a fairly normal life. For the first time since her marriage to Piggersnaff, she had not won a battle and Gingham had got his own way.

So it was in the Idiot household, that the desires of the offspring always caused commotion, tears and hundreds of arguments meaning that Jimmelta spent countless hours on the phone to her friends complaining about her family. How sad that an immeasurably, tastelessly, doughnut-y, rich woman should feel so unhappy and distraught with her lot.

And dear reader, what a sad day for all concerned – especially the Inherited Australian Convicts, who had really had enough of Jimmelta Chew Van Der Bratt and all the other Idiots in the family.

Something was brewing below the stairs, and they, the Inherited Australian Convicts, were not happy at all…

CHAPTER EIGHT

'Aw I've had enough of them ones upstairs – especially the Fat Doughy...' sniggered the oldest and wisest Inherited Australian Convict named Rooster, as he flexed his tremendous muscles which suddenly expanded to the size of a rugby ball. 'D'you know wha' we should do?' he whispered with the green in his eyes glinting and the tufts of grey hair gleaming out from the lobes of his long ears, curling round to the nape of his neck, bristling as he spoke. 'We should kidnap them all an' hold them to ransom...'

'What a brillian' idea Rooster! I am lovin' it!' cried One-Eared Lumpy (a name that we will talk about later). 'I'm just so bleedin' tired of cleanin' that revoltin' gold. I 'ate the stuff now, an' to fink I always loved nickin' it. Don' it change? D'you know, sometimes, jus' sometimes, I long for a cell, a meal served up for ya, a stint in a yard for an hour an' someone to make ya stay in yer cell... Lads, call me a dreamer, but is this a life workin' for a group of Idiots? I feel like I'm doin' life...' and thunderous applause resounded around the mouldy and damp-ridden kitchen. All the other hungry and badly kempt convicts agreed with One-Eared Lumpy.

This wasn't a life. This was doing life, except they didn't have to have shackles on their ankles.

'Well what are we gonna do then?' asked Pinky Squat, the ugliest, smallest, fattest but cleverest of the bunch. 'We could hijack them. Or,' he pondered, flicking some ear wax into the strawberry flan, 'we could make them into our slaves!' This stroke of genius created much enthusiasm and unusual excitement, as it wasn't often they had much to be happy about.

'Hang on one minute,' said Rooster, 'we ain't got enough. We'll have to call in the heavies an' get in buns to frighten them with.'

'BUNS, you mean GUNS!' replied One-Eared Lumpy.

"Ere, bags me the top of the table...' laughed Rooster, 'old age an' all.' The other two laughed. This could be great fun for them. How they hated working for the Idiots and how they loathed their greedy, selfish and tasteless existence.

'D'you know,' said One-Eared Lumpy, 'all the years I've been 'ere, I don't think they've been to an art gallery ONCE!! I've been to loads...'

'That's because you was casin' them up for the next job,' butted in Rooster, now quite enjoying the plan of attack. He'd certainly make them pay.

CHAPTER NINE

It was a normal day in Bullion Castle. The Inherited Australian Convicts were polishing the stairs, hallway and dining hall ready for the Idiots to have breakfast. The table was laid for the family and some of their local goats and other creatures. One by one, the family appeared on skates or anything fast, with the list of clothes they were wearing for the day. Each guzzled their favourite food whilst the hungry, thirsty Inherited Australian Convicts scrambled for each crumb that fell from the golden knives and forks to the antique golden floorboards.

'Well what have you got planned today?' quilled and trilled Jimmelta as she munched on her twentieth golden syrup and blackberry doughnut.

'We're learning how to fight in a war today,' said Gingham in a stout, firm sort of grown up way. As he spoke he brushed his crop of wild hair with a golden hairbrush, which Jimmelta found distressing because of his designer dandruff flicking into the food.

'Well that's incredibly important – darling who are you fighting?' she mused as she brushed her greasy hair with another golden brush. Of course, dear reader, hers was also designer and bespoke grease... However, all she wanted was a Cath Kidston one....

'The establishment to begin with...'

'Is that near Latvia? It's a long name for such a poor country, still I suppose they need one,' explored Jimmelta in her serious, deeply concerned voice, the one she saved for throwing out donations from her plane over arid stench-ridden climes. At this point Gingham turned his head incredulously, unable to believe how thick and stupid his mother really was. Did she really think 'Establishment' was a country or a state in Russia? He wondered what she would do if he joined the army or fought in some way for his homeland. He probably wouldn't tell her the truth. Gingham decided that, if this ever happened, he would say he was acting in a Hollywood blockbuster about the war. She'd like that, he thought.

'For God's sake Jimmelta! The boy is talking about bureaucracy in the army, you know, the red tape!' bellowed Piggersnaff looking up from his financial paper, horrified at his wife's lack of general intelligence.

'I didn't realise the army liked colours – red tape, darling I'm so impressed, it probably goes nicely with the uniforms. I suppose they keep the red tape locked away in bureaus for safe keeping. How terribly clever – especially for men – though I do think a woman must have chosen the colours.' She purred as she picked the middle of her doughnut. Everything always had an answer that always related to her own life, of course.

'We're OFF!' There was little point trying to explain the politics to their hapless and terminally hopeless mother, whose life and religion was dictated by the Church of Harvey Nichols. Wiping his lips with a golden napkin rather aggressively, Piggers picked up his golden leather briefcase and quickly made his exit, in such a rush a gust of wind trailed behind like a small frustrated tornado. His long dangly legs sped down the corridor, whilst a huge bony hand gesticulated into the air in horror and exasperation. All "she" had to do was read the paper, or listen to the news. That should be easy as he'd bought the TV stations for the children, just to entertain them. Thank God she hadn't needed to entertain NATO; though Piggers probably thought his hapless and hopeless wife would regard this as an abbreviation for a beauty cream or procedure. She did make him smile; she was a little daft at times, but he loved her.

'Remember children, whatever you do, DON'T GET IN TO TROUBLE AND DON'T WRITE!' screeched Jimmelta from the top of her golden table, from her golden chair. They all nodded, charged past the servants and got into their "small" but private shuttles. As they left Bullion, the Inherited Australian Convicts sniggered. They couldn't wait for "Doughy" to get off to her favourite place, the Church of Harvey Nichols, for a morning meeting with her other worthwhile and 'important' friends.

Piggersnaff went to his office to sort something out about Bolivia, his new acquisition; there was trouble with the natives and they were not happy. He had bought the country with some leftover loot from the sale of a couple of prisons. He was concerned as he wanted everyone in his new country to be happy and couldn't understand how some people were not settled.

One-Eared Lumpy was a little confused. He had thought that, with the help from the other Inherited Australian Convicts, breakfast would be a perfect time to kidnap the Idiots, so when the morning passed normally he was certainly puzzled.

'Fing is, One-Eared, we have to decide what we want to do with them,' responded Pinky Squat, climbing a ladder to clean the table. 'There's no point just taking them without deciding what fings we'll do...'

'Better be bleedin' awful since we've not had a meal, proper like, since the leftovers from the palace down the road. God I hate Piggersnaff's stupid gold. D'you know I've been shaving the legs of all the chairs and have two sacks of shavings now for the black market?'

'Naw, you mean "PINK MARKET Doughy sniggered Pinky Squat, thinking about Jimmelta's desire for soft colours.

'Don't she look like a doughnut?' responded Rooster, cleaning up the golden dishes from the long gleaming golden table.

'Aw I haven't seen a sight like it. She's like a squashy mountain, her waist must be... seventy inches, well, or something like that...' muttered One-Eared Lumpy, scraping the food from the floor after the usual food fight between the children.

'I'VE GOT IT! I KNOW WHAT WE'LL DO WITH THE IDIOTS!' roared Rooster, now laughing; and at that the other Inherited Australian Convicts felt as if somehow life was going to get just that little bit funnier!

CHAPTER TEN

Now that they had all fled for the day, Jimmelta decided to do something purposeful; today was going to be one for a good cause. As she sloped off to her enormous bedroom, passing the large gold-rimmed paintings of previous Idiots and Chew Van Der Bratts, it dawned on her how sad life was for most people, especially for herself. She wasn't content with the servants starving or curtseying as she slugged past. They had to call her Ma'am and wear white gloves, just like Dotty. Looking round at the sea of gold everywhere, tears came to her eyes. Piggers was so cruel not to let her have ONE Cath Kidston tablecloth or, well, any item would have done, it just wasn't fair.

Every day was the same. Piggers flew off to a new thing he'd bought – last week he'd put in a bid to buy the House of Loot. Actually, she didn't really care what he bought, as long as he kept away from her church – the Church of Harvey Nichols. As she got ready for her gold, fluffed bath, she wondered what people did, you know people, in shops. She wondered about where they lived, what sort of clothes they wore and whether they went to the same diamond mines for their shoes. Perhaps she should venture on to the streets incognito like a private detective.

She didn't know what to wear and consulted Dotty who immediately informed her that she had never got a tube on her own and went everywhere by carriage, and no she didn't use a taxi – ever – only because it was cheaper to use the royal limousine flanked by the cavalry. Anyway, she had to run because she was opening the new parliament and the whole new set of Members of Parliament had to be sworn in. More importantly, her horse was running in the 3.30 at Newmarket and she needed to get back to sort out her winnings. Gosh, thought Jimmelta, Dotty did have an action-packed day; maybe she could do the same, run a country or something. Perhaps she could pop over to Bolivia with Piggers

and do something useful, maybe set up an outlet or perfume counter, something people needed. She thought wistfully about conquering the earth and becoming a powerful magnate like the ones from the Spider's Web on TV.

CHAPTER ELEVEN

Dressed in black, Jimmelta crept out of the side door of Bullion Castle and onto the street which led down to the river bank. Aghast at the swarms of people and traffic frantically scurrying about their lives, she realised how fast the pace was on the street. She didn't need her black diamond-rimmed glasses as it was raining, so after taking them off, she didn't know what to do with them as normally one of the Inherited Australian Convicts would carry things for her. Stopping by a strange stand with lots of papers and a man huddled in a soaking coat, Jimmelta was horrified by the litter, and worse, the realisation that the heels on her shoes were not meant for walking. It was raining, the shoes were wrong, she'd forgotten her key back into Bullion Castle and she had run out of doughnuts, but thankfully she had her passport... that being her credit card.

Edging her way along the riverbank, being careful not to walk too fast in case the heels snapped, she made her way to a small alley where she could see a sign for footwear. Never in all her years had she entered a shop other than those in Knightsbridge, and even then, it was always with a body guard. Now, however, she was going into a tiny cheap shop asking for things called "Wellies".

'Eight quid doll,' quipped the smudged and red-eyed, wart-popping man shuffling to the rusty till which was overridden with sweet papers, coffee stains and crumpled up tissues. It had obviously seen better days.

'Ere doll, 'ave yer got something smaller than a hundred quid note? I've only got a fiver in me till, I ain't seen one of them for bleedin' years... Doll what does the ol' man do then?' quizzed the shop assistant, trembling as he held the hundred pound note; he didn't know whether to photocopy it, nick it, or find the right change. Sadly, like all decent people who are short on washing and social skills, he gave the note back. Something told him this fat, tasteless lady could be very important.

'Doll, I'm doing yer a favour; since it's the first sale of the day, you can 'ave them for free.'

'Gosh how kind, I won't forget this. Put these shoes into a plastic bag – careful, the heels are all black diamonds. The heels alone cost twenty thousand pounds...' And with that Jimmelta left the shop, wearing her wellies with pink and blue flowers and feeling like a million pounds. She knew that the day ahead was going to be one big adventure.

And it certainly was. Trying to get change for the hundred pound note proved quite a challenge; she couldn't comprehend why it kept getting shoved back in her face. Finally, after the fourteenth time of attempting to buy something, a busker at the Bank tube station told her it was a fake!

'WHAT? I don't do fake!' she screamed, then began to wonder in horror whether everything she had was fake, and that in reality the gold was fool's gold, that Bullion Castle was made of cardboard, and that Piggers didn't own Bolivia after all. Almost at the point of fainting at the thought of having to use the tube every day *and get a JOB,* Jimmelta decided she needed to get back to reality and so, blindly crying, she edged her way through the wet, soaked, dirt-ridden streets to the bottom of the Strand and to the side entrance of the castle. Fancy forgetting her key! 'I bet Dotty's never done this before,' she muttered to herself. What she still hadn't realised was the fact that Dotty had never needed to possess a key, touch a key or even use a key. When was the last time you saw a head of state opening the front door?

So once again dear reader we have an Idiot who now believes in fool's gold and, with a glimmer, a slither, a minute zillionth bit of intelligence, the first lady of Bullion Castle wondered how everything had happened. Ringing on the servants' bell she spoke through the intercom and waited for someone to let her in.

She waited and waited and waited, and then continued to wait and wait, with even more waiting. Naturally, as you and I both know, that whilst the Inherited Australian Convicts were not well fed, well versed, or well with anything, they could still hear – extremely well in fact. We know what they were all doing. Can you guess?

They were sitting, huddled over the intercom in the boot room, eating wheelbarrows of spicy chicken legs marinated in lemon and parsley crumbs, and banoffee pie smothered in the finest Jersey cream, washed down with the rarest black tea from China. There the servants sat, laughing at the pleading voice from outside which had risen to a hysterical cry for help.

'D'you know Rooster, I think it's raining really badly outside, in fact, there's talk of a storm,' purred One-Eared Lumpy, smiling at the image on camera of the ragged creature soaked to the skin, begging passers-by for a doughnut or the crust of salmon pie. 'Anything would do,' she yelped, 'even something from John Lewis or Marks and Spencer!' she declared to the rush hour commuters. They watched in amusement as she grabbed the coat tails of a gentleman in a suit and bowler hat.

'She has chosen well. Some posh geezer, nice tie... Awwww look AT THIS!' gasped Rooster. Open-mouthed they watched as the elegant business man took his umbrella and swiped Jimmelta across the back.

'Get out of the way you beggar, anyway, seems to me you're eating enough for ten by the looks of it!' and with that, he marched off with her clinging to his coat and trouser leg.

'Awwww,' whispered Rooster, wiping a tear from his eyes, 'aw, he didn't really mean that about bein' a beggar. So sad, so sad, aw aw aw soooooooo sad.' The others pulled their faces out of the banoffee pie and nodded in agreement.

'Let's see what she does next. Did she take her mobile?' queried Pinky Squat, worried that Piggersnaff could rescue her in their moment of triumph.

'Naw, she don't know how to use it, an' the little 'un threw it to some new lions they've bought. Makes up for us lot being eaten. We've got to make sure this works or else we'll be in the lion's fat gob,' said One-eared Lumpy, carelessly throwing a golden plate on the floor, delighted that it hadn't smashed.

'D'you know, once we've sorted this lot out, I never, never, never want to see a piece of bleedin' gold as long as I live. I 'ate the stuff. Give me a cell, four walls...' The others nodded. 'In fact, in future, when I get out of 'ere, I'm only gonna nick things that 'ave a bit of bleedin' taste!' The only positive thing about slaving for the Idiots was the Inherited Australian Convicts had learnt what *not* to do with money and how *not* to spend money.

But they couldn't wait to get their grubby, grizzly, nail-bitten paws on it! Actually, nor can we.

CHAPTER TWELVE

Let's go back to looking at the trials and tribulations of our very lovely Jimmelta who needed another doughnut fix and didn't know where to get one. For as long as memory served, she had always demanded and one would appear. Throughout the day in Bullion Castle, trolleys of different doughnuts straddled the golden corridors of power, ensuring that her guzzling, spot-blistered face was permanently stuffed.

'Actually,' commented the Inherited Australian Convict, 'it's well weird for someone obsessed with fashion and lookin' cool, you'd think she'd bleedin' well try starvin' herself an' chew on a bit of tha' bleedin'gold.' There was a nod and loud mutter of agreement amongst the amused convicts. The thought of the Fat Doughy swaying from foot to foot in the swarming crowds, being hustled and bustled, with the whale-like waist bubbling under her designer corset, with waves of white pulpy fat squeezing its way out of her bra and jumper, to nestle round the nape of her neck like a scarf, caused great hilarity for the onlookers in Bullion Castle.

'Aw d'you fink she'll get on a bus or a tube and get to the Church of Harvey Nichols?' sniggered Pinky Squat, supping the last drop of wine from the Idiots' world premier collection from the cellar.

'Ere, let's put on the camera an' track her down...' suggested Rooster, helping himself to a fistful of caviar, smoked salmon and tomato sauce. 'I bet she's in a bit of bovva now...' he said, licking his golden plate clean before throwing it on the floor.

They all peered through the lenses and saw Jimmelta walk up to innocent passers-by, grabbing them by their collars and demanding a doughnut or else. As she turned unknowingly towards the camera, the Inherited Australian Convicts saw two black eyes and her fat stretched over her head like a beret.

'She ain't 'avin' a good time with them commoners. Some are posher than her!' said One-Eared Lumpy, finishing off a recently cooked leg of organic and gentle lamb. It was at this point that they started to have a little sympathy as she was seen crawling on the pavement deliriously asking for a doughnut. Any would do, just as long as it was a doughnut. She was then asked by a policeman to move on and make sure she got a licence to beg as London was full of 'em. They did have a wave of sadness for her as she cried on her knees telling the policeman her husband probably could buy the whole police force and all she wanted was doughnut!

Too late. Jimmelta was dragged unceremoniously to a large police van, handcuffed and gagged to stop her wailing and disturbing the innocent passers-by with her dreadful behaviour. As she banged and screamed, two tired looking officers raised their eyebrows: this one looked like trouble. With that, they put the siren on full blast and turned the radio on as loudly as they could. And yet, to their disgust and horror... her scream overpowered the siren and the radio, too.

'She sounds like a whale in labour,' said one officer calmly, as he did the crossword. The other nodded in agreement.

'Actually, maybe this is what the dinosaurs sounded like. Maybe she's related to them...' chirped the second officer. Again they both sniggered: this one was trouble.

Stuffed in the back of the petrol-fumed van with only matted and flea-ridden hessian cloths to sit on, Jimmelta cried. Her day out mixing with the rest of the people was now turning out like something from a horror story – similar to being made to shop in 'Pound and Pence Only'.   Her mind was going mad...

WHERE WERE THE SERVANTS?

DIDN'T THEY KNOW SHE WANTED TO GET BACK HOME?

WHERE WAS EVERYONE WHEN SHE NEEDED THEM?

WHY DIDN'T PEOPLE WASH OR WEAR BRIGHT CLOTHES?

WHERE WERE THE SERVANTS WHEN SHE NEEDED THEM?

WHY WERE THERE SO MANY STALE AND DIRTY PEOPLE?

AND THE PEOPLE, SOME SMELT AND THEY WEREN'T EVEN FRENCH!

CHAPTER THIRTEEN

Back in Bullion Castle, the Inherited Australian Convicts were preparing for the children to come home from school. All, that is, except for Kidston who had been with a series of nannies all day teaching him how to talk in goat, something that Piggersnaff still insisted upon for all the children.

It was the tornado-like sound of the small personalised shuttles arriving on the roof of the castle and the formidable sound of the three children carelessly making their way into the grounds that made the golden pirates realise the end of the day was near. They had been so mesmerised by the spectacle of Jimmelta being taken by the police for disturbing the peace, over her need for a doughnut, and the outcry it had caused, that everyone had forgotten about the children, and worse still, they hadn't yet decided how to punish them!

It was easy. The three children were going to polish EVERYTHING! 'That should do it, we'll get them to bleedin' polish all the gold an' then the cobwebs, an' then the floors an' knives' an' forks...'

'What about cookin'? We could do wiv a nice roast dinna or summit,' chuckled Pinky Squat. 'All this hostagin' makes us 'ungry, realllllly 'ungry,' he sighed, rubbing his stomach longingly. The others laughed in glee at the thought of the precocious Idiots cleaning and polishing the gold. Each wondered how long it would take them to do three golden chairs each. Perhaps a bet should be placed on the winner.

'So what's the prize for the winner?' asked One-Eared Lumpy, finishing off a whole trifle with a bucketload of double cream.

'The luxury of 'aving a luverly bowl of hot oats an' salt' replied Rooster. 'AND for the others... EVEN MORE POLISHING! WHAT ABOUT THE STAIRS?' The other Inherited Australian Convicts roared with laughter, their bloated stomachs gurgling up and down, squishing, squashing and slibbering to the rhythm of the chortling bellies.

'We need a chain for 'em so they don't escape,'

pondered Pinky, looking around for some inspiration, finding nothing in the kitchen. 'I 'ave an excellent idea. If we go to Fat Doughy's bedroom we'll get some of her belts and chains an' use them.'

'But we won't 'urt them too much will we Pinky?' quizzed One-Eared Lumpy, a bit concerned about what Piggers might do to them once it was all over.

'Nah. We'll jus' let 'em know what's like to be a convict an' a servant,' replied Pinky, scanning the place for anything resembling a chain to use on the delightful young Idiots. Well, you can imagine how excited these poor, sad, undernourished and uneducated Inherited Australian Convicts felt. Ever since they had swum back from the Atlantic, gasping for food, water and shelter, their lives had been anything but wonderful. Rather than celebrate their survival, Piggers and Jimmelta immediately gave them a death-defying list of chores and jobs to do around the castle, with an hourly itinerary included. And, rather than give them a bath, the Idiots made them darn and stitch any ragged ends of material on their clothes.

This was time for their revenge – and boy was it going to be good!

Before we get ourselves stuck into what happens in Bullion Castle, I think we should have a sneaky look to see how our own 'very lovely' Jimmelta is coping with the horrors of civilian life behind bars in a cell inside Soho Police Station. Dear readers, if there is one place in London where one should take security seriously, other than Hackney Wick, it has to be Soho. Of course she'd heard of all the gang robberies around the place, knifings, muggings and disorderly behaviour, but never in all her life had she been here.

As you would expect, the surroundings of the police station were not exactly the next best thing to a five-star hotel. The road leading up to the entrance was dirty. Litter scattered everywhere, scuffed and broken doors, windows and smashed-in cars indicated to Jimmelta that this really wasn't the place to come shopping. Every so often there was someone strewn on the pavement or stuffed in the doorway of a derelict shop trying to keep warm and dry. Adding to this, there seemed to be a wild cat and dog population which roamed the area scouring for food in mangled and putrid bins, all snarling and spitting as they devoured any spare scraps. Jimmelta scanned the place through a mist of tears, dribbling eye makeup and a soggy running nose: she wouldn't be mentioning this at the Church of Harvey Nichols – not to anyone.

'Listen luv yer can't break the law over a doughnut. It ain't right,' said the policeman behind the grubby, sick-stained, kebab-ridden desk. 'Blimey, you'd think that you'd like to fight over a nice bit of lettuce or tomato. Hasn't any one told yer luv? You look like a doughnut. Honest to God luv, I'm doin' yer a favour,' and with that the paunchy black-headed copper stuffed the last bit of strawberry doughnut into his greasy mouth whilst Jimmelta screamed at the top of her voice as her bag was being emptied for terrorist bombs.

'Leave this alone you piece of nylon vermin! This is a bespoke Snotta De Grassa Bag made from the entrails of designer bats and chickens! It takes three years for one to mature and YOU! YOU! YOU...! How dare you use my Lip-a-Lot-Stick-a-Lot Lipstick that comes from the rarest lips of chipmunks!' Tears poured down her dirty mascara-smeared face, dropping into puddles in the roll of fat squelching around the nape of her neck like a scarf.

'So let's see, your name is Jimmelta Chew Van Der Bratt...' PC Clacker-Hammer said as he delved into the shiny sparkling purse lying on the desk along with all of Jimmelta's other possessions.

'Careful! You sweaty, sniffling, nylon, black-headed policeman! That's encrusted in South African black diamonds!' she yelled, spitting as she spoke, spraying Clacker-Hammer with designer and bespoke saliva.

'IT'S BESPOKE…!'

'Really, I didn't know purses spoke,' replied Clacker-Hammer, now smiling at her incandescent rage, knowing he had a real nutter here, and thinking boy was he gonna milk it!

'STUPID BONGO-FACED, LIZARD-DROPPING, CURD-LACED IDIOT! THE PURSE WAS SPECIALLY MADE FOR ME! ONLY DOTTY'S GOT ONE!'

Poor Jimmelta was about to explode with such anger at the stupidity of the man. Didn't he know quality when he saw it? Still, anyone who saw nylon, dared to own it, or had the misfortune to wear it… NEEDED HELP!

So I am going to leave this spectacle in Soho Police Station in the knowledge that our lovely Jimmelta was truly suffering and, possibly, learning to get on with others less fortunate than herself. Tragically, as with most disgustingly spoilt and atrociously badly behaved people, she thought this spell "be'ind bars" was the worst thing in the world. The truth of the matter was, dear reader, that she was right.

CHAPTER FOURTEEN

'Here they come!' mouthed Pinky Squat to the others down the corridor as the hurricane of noise descended into the castle and the three unruly children gnawed their way through countless chocolate bars placed strategically towards the main room near the dining hall. Throwing wrapping paper after wrapping paper on the floor, leaving a trail of muddy shoes and boots, the guzzling trio, quite unaware of any differences in their environment, made their way to the main room and promptly put on the TV.

'Paisley, ring for the Homework Convict and get him to bring all the subject books. Oh and tell him he has to read six chapters from one. Mother's so stupid, she doesn't understand that some bright people write!' And with that, Gingham checked the room before getting out his new biro, something he had to keep hidden from his parents. Paisley dutifully nodded and rang for an Inherited Homework Convict for secondary education and got back to playing with the family goats. After a while Gingham began to get a little impatient. Why were they taking so long? What were they doing?

84

Why was it so quiet? Why wasn't their mother shouting for another doughnut?

As they waited for an Inherited Homework Convict, a lashing of chains clashing on to the finest marble floors grew louder and nearer. There in the entrance of the large room stood the Inherited Australian Convicts with chains, ties and polishing equipment on a long trolley ready for the fun.

'Yer muther's not 'ere she went outside...'

'What?' reported Polka, horrified. 'Mummy HATES other people. If they aren't wearing Swottas and Nottas, or boots by Larda or Sneeze Ent Florets... even Dotty knows what she's like,' she pondered, guzzling an enormous piece of cake, on, of course, a golden plate.

'Well we've 'ad her hijacked and she's in the clink in Soho for screamin' for more bleedin' doughnuts. So this is it, you lizard-lazy spot-bellied greasy-scummed brats!' yelled Pinky Squat, charging at the three children who, till this point, were quite bemused. This was until the other Inherited Australian Convicts slammed down their working overalls and produced the cleaning cloths and grease for polishing the mountains of gold.

'I'm not wearing THIS!' bellowed Gingham. 'It is not linen or cotton...'

'Get it on your bleedin' fat arse now or I'll smash your spoilt pig-like nose in it an' make it into a plate!' bawled Rooster,

quite enjoying seeing the children crying as they put the overalls on over their clothes.

'Wait till Mummy gets home!' snarled Polka, struggling with the buttons, 'she'll have you eaten by the goats or lions!'

'Listen material face-chub-a-lot, you's goin' to polish an' polish an' polish – with this chain on!' roared Rooster, laughing as he watched the children look strangely at the tin of grease.

'Is this,' said Paisley slowly, 'a new sport? I haven't heard of it and I think this should be jolly good fun.' The Inherited Australian Convicts glared at him. This was meant to be a punishment. It hadn't crossed their minds that the Idiots, being true to their name, might find the hostage experience exciting.

'Paisley are you being stupid? They are taking us HOSTAGE!' screamed Polka, stamping her foot and trying to kick Rooster, who was paying little attention.

'Right you lot, this is the cleanin' stuff an' 'ere are the cloths!' With that, One-Eared Lumpy threw the cloths at the spoilt lizard-like Idiots, who began crying and screaming as they began cleaning the long golden table.

After half an hour of polishing, grease everywhere, in most cases not on the table, Gingham demanded a drink of water.

'Fat Doughy won't let us 'ave one until we've finished the job. Same applies here,' laughed Rooster, settling himself in for the night. This lot were going to take bleedin' ages at this rate. So to soften the blow, he poured himself another glass of vintage wine, costing thousands of pounds of course, and had a leg of organic lamb with freshly cut mint. Meanwhile, to pass the time, Pinky Squat was swinging from the diamond chandeliers with a bucket of chicken wings watching Polka scream in fear and anger.

'This is the ONLY DIAMOND CHANDELIER in the WHOLE WORLD! MUMMY'S GOING TO KILL YOU!' Tears of rage ran down her pallid face as she watched treasured diamonds falling to the ground like sprays of fairy dust casting a magical spell, each one glistening with hope. It certainly was hope – One-Eared Lumpy was sweeping them up and collecting the fragments in a bucket titled "Dimonds on'y" – yes spelling had never been their strong point when in prison. Rooster could see traits of Jimmelta in Polka and he didn't like them.

'Aw you can 'ave one from Dotty's pad up the road, she might even give you her crown or some fing, yer never know…' chortled Pinky Squat, now sitting on Piggersnaff's golden chair.

'Right you's lot 'urry up, you've got the whole table to do an' the chairs. No food till it's done!' he yelled, standing on the table pretending to do a tap dance.

'Wait till my father sees this!' bawled Gingham. 'He's going to have you sent back to prison to a high security wing! HOW DARE YOU RUIN OUR BEAUTIFUL PALACE!' Gingham screamed as he tried to polish a chair; how his hands hurt and how he needed a drink of water. How he wanted to escape from these evil convicts.

Actually, dear reader, as we know, the revolting convicts were NOT revolting; it was the Idiot's treatment of the convicts that was revolting, repugnant and, of course, rude. How we want the convicts to enjoy teaching these young Idiots a lesson, one that just might, just might, change them into decent people for the future. Anyway, we must get back to watching the three elder Idiots scrubbing away, polishing the tasteless table, their sweaty, pallid brows seeping with grease, gunk and blackheads as they worked.

Isn't it strange how a little bit of work starts to change people? You have to remember, the three

eldest had never wiped a surface, opened a bottle of cleaner, used a grease-worn cloth and rubbed until a surface began to sparkle. It must have been the third hour of the polishing when Polka noticed how the light shone on the smooth golden surface of the table, allowing her to see her reflection, which, for the first time ever, had a pinky warm glow from the strenuous effort required to clean the daily dirt and grime after each meal. As she rubbed off the hardened remnants of poached egg, congealed porridge, jam and treacle, Polka was suddenly annoyed at the mess left throughout the day.

'There! This is starting to look really good! See this?' she said, proudly pointing to her part of the sparkling table showing the lounging convicts as they guzzled Jimmelta's private doughnut collection from Harrods' Food Pile. However, even though Polka was starting to quite enjoy the novelty of being a prisoner, she wasn't quite sure whether the thought of cleaning every day was what she wanted. Gingham on the other hand, slammed and stamped on the table, screamed at the increasingly fat Inherited Australian Convicts who were shovelling exotic foods into their dirty, infested, slime-ridden mouths, quaffing wine and anything they could lay their hands on.

'Ere, don' miss out on anyfing, it all gotta shine, or else there'll be trouble!' snarled One-Eared Lumpy as he ate the final stack of special doughnuts laced with chocolate ice cream drizzled with cream. Rubbing his fat sponge-like stomach, he commanded Paisley to pass him even more food. Crying, his nose dribbling, his soft gentle hands sore and red from the scrubbing and rubbing, he gathered the strength to slither a pile of chocolate to him.

'Come on you lazy spoilt wretch, move faster!' Paisley's little squidgy legs bobbled towards the now bloated Inherited Australian Convict who was picking his nose. It was a disgusting sight to behold, the servants all lying around the dining hall, scoffing their food and whipping the Idiots every now and then to make them work. All three were now suffering badly and needed to eat and drink. For the first time ever, Gingham wanted to do his homework! Polka wanted to clean her room and Paisley wanted to sort out all his games! Anything other than this horrible existence. They huddled over the cleaning cloths whilst their work was checked.

This really wasn't fair, why should they have to clean their own house? But as we the readers know, when children are so utterly disgustingly rude, spoilt and above all greedy, there comes a time when lessons have to be learnt. Just to add salt to their wounds, the Inherited Australian Convicts decided to act like the young Idiots and have juice and food, but leave a trail everywhere.

The children screamed in horror as they saw all their hard work carelessly messed up without a thought. They were reminded: 'This is 'ow you lot act all the time!' snapped Rooster, who was deciding how long they would play games with this lot. He suddenly thought, they hadn't seen the lovely Piggersnaff this evening and wondered what had happened to him. They'd also forgotten to see how Kidston was doing in the airing cupboard (they'd left him there with some baby rusks and rattles). Since they all quite liked the baby, it had been decided to keep him safe, and the airing cupboard seemed to be the answer.

CHAPTER FIFTEEN

I think we should get back and see what has happened to Jimmelta, for as we know, she was having a tough time in the outside world. Inside the dingy tobacco-stained station, mould clung to damp walls in large globular rolls and the long sparsely furnished corridor walls were filled with numerous posters for wanted and caught criminals. As she mindlessly walked to her new home, Jimmelta passed row upon row of people locked behind bars screaming, yelling, crying and demanding help. Not only did they sound like something out of a freak show, this she could cope with; it was worse, much worse. They smelt very, very badly and as she plugged up her delicate nose with her now grubby fingers, Jimmelta vowed that if she should ever become prime minister, soap would be given to all prisoners, along with sweet-scented deodorant. This really was a new world.

A new world to which Jimmelta was not suited at all.

It was a world which she did not intend to belong to – at any cost. Making her way to a large overcrowded cell, Jimmelta prayed that nobody would ever find out about this. She would, she decided, pay every single blackmail threat… forever and ever and ever.

Sitting slouched on the only broken stool in a heaving prison cell, she whimpered and cried into her final soft scented tissues about the impending misery she was about to endure with the law. She noticed as she scanned the small, infested, stench-infused area, that there were pockets of litter brimming with soft putrid pus, clogged with flies, ants, cockroaches, sweet packets, tissues, leftover food, toe nails, matted hair brush bristles and make-up pads. She decided this must be the nearest place to hell. Crying once again, for her own tragedy and that of the deathly smell, Jimmelta vowed once she got home and spoke to Piggers, that she would donate soap to every prison cell in England, along with soft fresh towels from the Church of Harvey Nichols.

Her altruistic thoughts were squashed by other inmates pounding the hatch in the door for the only food of the day. Bemused and unaware of the limited rations of food, our very own Idiot, shocked by the complete lack of manners, assumed this was just the starters. Once the plate had been devoured of its stale contents, it was slung to one side of the room and everyone went back to sleep or chatting. Noting the empty plate, Jimmelta took it to the hatch opened it, peered out and demanded to see an officer.

'We're waiting for the main course and since there is no menu, you will have to tell me what's on today...' Gingerly holding her shoes up into the air and counting how many diamonds were left, Jimmelta turned and asked a small, skinny, heavily tattooed woman if there was any way she could get some food. The woman was looking puzzled at the actions, nodded and gave a sneering smile. Whilst doing this, Jimmelta polished each one left in the heels, letting the pathetic little skinny wizened woman know she had a bartering tool. The woman nodded and edged closely to this new rich inmate and pointed at the diamonds, which sparkled like splintered stars in the downtrodden and grubby heels.

'Depends what's in it for me, but I can help you if ya like? 'Course it's got to be worth my while... If you know what I mean,' she whispered, pointing once again at the shoes and in particular the heels.

Jimmelta nodded, there was a little bit of hope in this place after all.

'HA HA AHA!' roared the policemen, holding their sides as they laughed, for they knew this was the only meal and that it had all gone.

'Lady, this was the first, second, third an' fourth course!' said one of the men, crying with laughter at the request; this woman was an absolute scream. When Jimmelta realised that this was really it, there wouldn't be any more food for the day, she meekly went back to her stool and cried.

'Listen love, that was a real good thing you did for us, but this is how it works until we get bail…'

'BAIL?' retorted Jimmelta, 'I DON'T NEED BAIL, I'M NOT A CONVICT!' Suddenly she had a vision of herself wearing one of the Inherited Australian Convict's uniforms from Bullion Castle and this made her shudder – not once, twice, or three times, but continually throughout the day. How she wished for her family, Piggers, clean soap, fresh clothes and JUST three OR four doughnuts. Had her life in the space of one day fallen into such disrepute and trauma, without any hope of a reprieve, all for a doughnut in a London street? Her stomach, nearly six feet of it,

rumbled with hunger like a thunder storm over a small island, shaking the others in its wake. Embarrassed by the noise, she began to explain that she had a gentle disposition but was sharply interrupted.

'More like a fat disposition love!' heckled a voice from the other side of the cell. It was met with a sea of laughter and sniggers. Nobody in Bullion Castle had ever mentioned her weight or expanding waistline. Nobody had ever criticised her about the layers of flesh slobbering off her frame. Nobody had even thought to question her eating habits in Bullion Castle; she thought she was beautiful. So the sneering and guttural comments were not only horrifying to her, but also a rude awakening to the cruelty of the outside world. If only someone had informed her that a waistband of seventy was just a little on the large size, she might have cut down on her doughnuts and eaten the odd apple.

'Just fink love, all them doughnuts 'ave given yer that loverrrly waist! Yer could use this time in the clink as an 'ealth farm!' An uproar of laughter echoed throughout the station. Realising that she would be better just to keep quiet and shut up, for the first time in her whole life Jimmelta did just that. She stayed quiet and still, longing to be back home, sitting at her golden table with its golden chairs.

This was all a far cry from her current abode.

As evening began to close in on the station, many of the women cramped in the cells found places and began to fall asleep. Everyone except our Jimmelta, who needed to have a shower. Calling to the policeman on duty through the hatch she asked gingerly for some soap, a towel and a place to have a shower. Flabbergasted and amused the duty men ushered her out into the passageway where the echo of wails, yells and arguments consumed the area. True to form, she was concerned about her shoes, as the diamonds had started cracking and the last thing she wanted was other prisoners knowing she had these stuck in her heels. Carefully, she sneaked her way through the litter and debris stacked outside each cell and followed the men. After what seemed like hours, they arrived at a large steel door studded with barbed wire. Immediately she questioned whether this was a new design of door, obviously not one she'd seen in the Church of Harvey Nichols, interesting though. Suddenly she was catapulted out in to an enormous concrete space, bare of anything except barbed wire. Confused and slightly worried she said, 'Look I only want a shower…'

'And 'ere you are m'lady!' With that the policemen took a fire hose and sprayed her with high pressure water. Ducking and diving from the cascades of water, Jimmelta cried at its coldness, cried for the ruin of her Helmit Twang top and trousers, cried for her hand-picked diamond, snakeskin and palladium shoes. But above all, she bawled her eyes out for not having scented soap, a clean towel and a fresh soft robe to wear to bed. Little did she know there weren't any beds, just other people to lie on!

So the nightmare continued until it fell dark, and then the water halted. She was ushered inside, dripping wet, her clothes paddling like the fins of a dolphin. One of the cops threw her a tea towel and shouted, 'Ere love, a towel for yer, it's all we got.' Gratefully she grabbed it and dried herself as best she could. Feeling sorry for her, they let her use the visitors' toilets where, to her amazement, she found soft warm towels with some clean garments.

'Thought you might find these useful,' said one of the older policemen, who actually felt sorry for her, realising that she wasn't quite the same as the others in her cell. 'Have you phoned your lawyer love? So you can get bail – that's money for you to pay so you can get 'ome t'night.' She shook her head; somehow her arrogant behaviour would not work here and she knew she needed help.

Well reader, I think something was happening to Jimmelta, don't you? She wasn't the same person who had sneaked out of the house early in the morning looking for a little adventure!

CHAPTER SIXTEEN

B ack at Bullion Castle, the Inherited Australian Convicts were having the time of their lives. After making the spoilt repugnant Idiots clean the castle – without any food or water – the grubby, grizzly, spot-breaking, snot-ridden children were pushed out on the court yard and pegged up on the washing line along with their clothes. Of course, dear reader, possibly one of the greatest things about living in a grotesquely tasteless golden castle was that nobody could hear you scream or shout. Can you picture the scene? The three young workers, now so sweaty, smelly and greasy from hard labour, were hung by pegs by their clothes on the washing line and were yelling at the top of their voices.

And what a marvellous sight it was, as nobody could hear them or see them!

What a wonderful sight and how the Inherited Australian Convicts laughed as they guzzled food, wine and smoked Piggers' vintage cigars.

'Well lads, I think we'll go inside an' leave 'em for a few hours; let's say till after it's dark…' smiled Rooster, blowing circles of smoke into the air as he lounged on a seat sipping a rather nice 1975 claret.

'What if it rains?' asked One-Eared Lumpy, just a little concerned about the wellfare of the younger children.

'They'll get wet an' 'ave a nice long shower won't they!' chortled Rooster, watching in delight at the sight of the Idiots kicking, screaming, waving their arms about and, of course, crying.

Time passed, the clouds came down, the darkness replaced daylight, the moon replaced the sun, owls replaced the blackbirds, the whimpers from the washing line replaced the roaring and crying. One by one, the children fell asleep on the line, the pegs sticking into their clothes, each had found some way to try and gain comfort. All wanted to go to the toilet, but nobody mentioned it just in case something happened.

They would have been brought in earlier, but the convicts had eaten so much, drunk so much, and laughed so much, that they fell asleep and it was only when the television made a pinging noise that they woke up. They wanted to shock the children – not kill them! When they reached the courtyard, each convict was secretly pleased that it hadn't rained as they watched the children being held together by pegs on the line. Lowering it down, the children, who now didn't seem quite so fat, so repulsive, so spoilt, so demanding, were ushered into the castle and led to their bedrooms.

'Ere, why are we being so bleedin' nice? We're meant to be givin' them 'ard times!' exclaimed One-Eared Lumpy as he pulled the boots off Gingham who was snoring with his arms stuck up in the air.

'Well lads, there's always tomorrow. Can't wait to see Fat Doughy,' laughed Rooster. The evening had exceeded his expectations and he was determined to have some more. As the evening drew to a close, the children, for the first time ever, appreciated soft clean bedding, fresh clothes and some simple things such as soap and water. The Inherited Australian Convicts finished the evening snuggled up in sumptuous guest suites, where they relished bathing in large golden baths with overflowing bubbles, whilst the televisions blasted full pelt. Finally, each fell asleep in deep cloud-like duvets which cuddled them into their dreams.

Little has been said about Piggersnaff, who normally came home each night, but for some reason, after a "phone call" from the Bolivian Government about the discovery of a gold mine in the mountains, had decided to stay away for a few days. Finding the mine proved to be difficult and Bolivian officials were confused about the phone call. So Piggers, determined to find it, grabbed some natives and donkeys and headed for the mountains with dreams of discovering more gold. For the time being we shall leave him to explore for treasure and return to the hostage takeover in Bullion Castle.

Strangely enough, as morning broke in Bullion Castle, and whilst the Inherited Australian Convicts snored heavily after the previous day, odd behaviour was emerging from the children's bedrooms. Gingham dragged himself out of bed quickly, had a shower, AND then proceeded to CLEAN it! The trauma of the previous day had made him realise how selfish a person he was, and worse, how unpleasant, fat, demanding and self-centred his life had made him. Of course, dear reader, we know that this holier-than-thou attitude would probably only last a day or so, but it was a start. Feeling quite pleased with himself, even smug, Gingham woke the other Idiots up and insisted that they too cleaned their rooms.

Actually, the main reason was he was scared of being put out on to the washing line again and housework seemed the better option.

'Do you think we should make the IACs a cup of tea?' asked Paisley, puffing up his bed pillows. 'I mean although yesterday was really disgusting and horrid, I hated cleaning up the mess all the time in the dining hall.' The other two nodded in agreement. This new splurge of domestication resulted from an innate fear of being asked to polish the entire furniture in the castle. All dreaded the days it would take just to get through a few rooms. The children froze at the thought and quickly began to prepare breakfast. Polka would make toast, whilst Paisley and Gingham would make tea.

'I actually grew to quite like the polishing,' added Polka, sheepishly trying to find coat hangers for her mounds of clothes that were strewn around the room.

'Thing is,' said Gingham cagily, 'We've never made a cup of tea before. I don't know where stuff is kept, though I know it's in the kitchen,' he muttered.

Something had happened. All three young Idiots, now neatly and cleanly dressed, quietly and secretly shuddered at the thought of spending another night pegged to the washing line, especially if it rained. In the kitchen, after struggling with the amount of tea in a cup and using the kettle and after some turbulence, their FIRST cuppa was ready. Yes I know, you and I have been making cups of tea and coffee for as long as we can remember; but you must understand these children had been so disgustingly spoilt they even had Inherited Australian Convicts buttering their toast for them! So this, dear reader, was a major breakthrough, in addition to their clean and tidy bedrooms.

Rooster was surprised at the knock on the door with a head peeping round to wake him with a cup of rather milky tea; nevertheless, he gasped at Polka standing there by the bed smiling.

'Bleedin' 'ell what's this?' yawned Rooster, thinking he was dreaming. He'd never in all the time at Bullion Castle seen any of the Idiots make a kind gesture towards other people. It was almost unheard of!

'Well Rooster, I thought for once I'd bring you tea in bed. Gingham's making breakfast in the kitchen. It'll be ready in ten minutes – I think.' With that, she promptly turned and left, leaving a flabbergasted Rooster unable to comprehend what had taken place.

So, the Inherited Australian Convicts all had breakfast served to them by the three young Idiots who struggled with making toast, tea and nearly burnt Bullion Castle when trying to fry sausages. Of course, we have forgotten to mention Kidston, who had moved from the airing cupboard to under the table in the dining hall and was quite content playing with pots and pans.

As they were eating, One-Eared-Lumpy muttered, 'Fought we was gonna give 'em another day like yesterday…' as he was shovelling bacon and eggs into his mouth. 'Listen men, we've got a result! What more d'you want? AND breakfast!' replied a shocked Rooster.

CHAPTER SEVENTEEN

And so dear readers, it came to pass that in the course of one sharp horrid day instigated by the Inherited Australian Convicts, three thanklessly spoilt, greasy, undesirable kids turned into fairly decent human beings. Once Gingham got his head around the cooking thing and organised the kitchen, One-Eared-Lumpy showed him how to make the kangerbarra snarra hamburger (Australian of course), thereby wowing the family. In fact, in a short space of time Gingham was turning into a culinary whizz; his boiled eggs were excellent. It seems strange that a group of servants should train the children, and not their over indulgent parents, who still continued to believe that anything dressed in gold was the answer.

However, the Inherited Australian Convicts were not quite ready to forgive Jimmelta, who was still waiting for bail in Soho jail, and who had been given the thankless job of cleaning out the dirt from the cells each day. There were benefits to this slavery; Jimmelta had almost lost the double or triple fat from her neck, her waist had whittled down to sixty inches and she had learnt not to change her clothes every hour. And it was so long since she had eaten one doughnut, she dreamt of them in her jail clothes. Her diamond shoes, downtrodden, were now diamond-less, as she'd had to pick them out of the heels for bribery in the pecking order behind bars. As much as she missed her life and, of course, her children, she wondered if they would begin to regard their mother as a distant memory, for whilst she had only been gone for days, it felt like months.

Another rainy day drew to a close when the policeman on duty shouted into her cell, which she shared with twenty, sweaty, dirty, rather rough other women.

'Chew Van Der Bratt! You are to appear before court tomorrow for reckless behaviour over a doughnut. Time: TEN THIRTY. BE READY!' With that, the sound of heavily nailed hobnailed boots disappeared down the corridor. Jimmelta sank into her bug-infested sack, scratched her legs for the millionth time and cried. One by one, all her inmates had either been released or put in jail and she was just left holding her shoes, now diamond-less, with nothing in the world except for the memories of her former life. She cried as she looked at the dirt and squalor of the cells and decided that once she was free she was going to change. Not for her, the world of charities or doing "good", either. No, she was going to eat the finest food, dress in the finest clothes and bathe in the finest oils. Strangers to her castle would be scanned for smells and dirty clothes and she was going to insist on the children changing three times a day. Never ever again, was she going to live in such a repugnant environment, or have those close to her not be clean. After that, she would think about helping a charity or something. Anything; as long as it was clean.

All she wanted was a bath with clean soft towels... Oh, and a range of warm doughnuts oozing with jam, cream and custard. Not a lot.

CHAPTER EIGHTEEN

The judge was a small, wrinkly, hook-nosed old man who had great trouble hearing what was going on and every so often asked members of the court about Chelsea Football Club, which, as you can imagine, had nothing to do with each case. As Jimmelta watched the defendants stand one by one before the court, she realised how, in a short space of time, her life had spiralled into an abyss of street crime. Now, she was only as good as her last diamond.

'Chew Van Der Bratt!' At this announcement she stood up with her hands cuffed behind her back.

Her legs were burning to be itched, the diamond-less heels of her shoes were downtrodden and she smelt. Not of some exotic fragrance, but of sweat and dirt-ridden clothes that had a lingering odour similar to that of a rotten fish simmering in rat-infested shoes. This was not from the designer section in Harvey Nichols.

'Well well well,' chirped the judge, looking at the defendant. 'You're one of the Idiots, aren't you? I know Piggersnaff's father. Has he still got the goats? Why are you here?' He mumbled as he glanced around the court. Most people were reading, chewing, talking or sleeping; he had to do something about this behaviour as people never listened to his cases. Once again he asked about Chelsea Football Club at which Jimmelta had to shake her head; those sorts of things never really interested her.

'Do you know something?' boomed the judge, 'This is the first time EVER I have had to charge anyone for assault over a doughnut! How greedy is that? Anyway, have you got anything to say other than that you were hungry?'

She looked up to the imposing bench where he sat and as she whispered, 'No,' a tear trickled down her face; not because of the shame, but because she thought of how she'd had to barter with the diamonds in the heels of her shoes. Had her life in such a short space of time been reduced to this horrible existence – and where was Piggers?

The booming voice of the judge interrupted her pitiful thoughts. 'Chew Van Der Bratt, I sentence you to sixty days community service on the stalls at Blackpool Illuminations. One day for each inch of your waist!' A gasp of shock rumbled around the courtroom, interspersed with sniggers and giggles at the thought of this doughnut-stuffed, leaden lump working on a cold, damp, dirty stall, having to beg for people to spend money. Jimmelta bolted upright on hearing the sentence. Surely she could just build him a new court or speak to Dotty about a knighthood? There must be something she could buy or do rather than have to suffer the indignity of working on a fair stall in a freezing cold place like Blackpool?

'Your Honour, could we strike a deal? How about I build you a new court or speak to my neighbour about a knighthood? Anything rather than this sentence!'

'How dare you even think about trying to bribe me? This could be ANOTHER OFFENCE,' screamed the judge, hurling his wig at her whilst roaring with rage. 'Don't you understand? Nobody is above the law! NOT EVEN YOU!'

Now you and I know how the law works dear reader. You get sentenced; your name is in the paper, people tut as they read about you. Then you're forgotten; behind bars. Of course that happens in the millions and zillions of cases all over the world – that is except for Jimmelta. As word reached the press about this futile case going to court, they, like scavengers, sniffed out as much information as possible. By the time the bedraggled old judge was due to pass sentence, the court was heaving with reporters and publicity agents.

As this drama continued to unfold, newspapers and TV stations were now giving this rather small, meaningless, stupid case huge coverage, with headlines in the national papers and main TV channels. Already publicity agents were phoning the court to work on behalf of Jimmelta, and the mogul of all publicity agents, MOTO Mouth, was ready to cut a deal with the Idiots and, of course, the judge. As the sentence was being passed again, the policeman by the witness box handed our very own convict the phone.

Just the chaos of this case was enough to keep the papers in headlines, with Jimmelta the lead star; something she had always yearned for. BUT NOT LIKE THIS!

CHAPTER NINETEEN

'It's MOTO MOUTH! He's big; he handles all the big names in the showbiz world! He's probably going to handle your time at the Illuminations! Quick while the judge is going mad,' he whispered to her, 'he does this for about five minutes at the end of cases he likes…' With that, a small policeman with warts on his nose handed Jimmelta the phone. She nodded. The whole of her life was like something out of horror movie, only getting worse.

'Is that Jimmelta? MOTO Mouth here! Just to say I'll handle the publicity for this! We'll make a fortune babe. Film rights, interview rights. We'll have world exclusives in magazines such as Fluff and the new big one, Face Lift. You alright with that babe? We'll get a few headlines from Bullion Castle with the kids, see how they're coping, and a one-off with Piggersnaff in his new country. IS THAT OK? My chief guy will take you by limousine to Blackpool, nice place… See you babe.' With that, the conversation ended promptly, well actually, it was a one-sided conversation, Jimmelta, saying nothing – a rare event. Onlookers from the gallery stared open-mouthed at the chaos and frenzy surrounding the case. There hadn't been

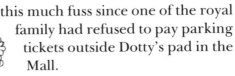 this much fuss since one of the royal family had refused to pay parking tickets outside Dotty's pad in the Mall.

As she thought about her previous life, Jimmelta hung her head. Things couldn't be worse... Blackpool Illuminations... Cold, damp, dirty mud... Perhaps she could have her sentence changed; a stint in jail where she could write a book, her memoirs. Then she remembered... She couldn't write, she couldn't even recall the complete alphabet (only the most popular letters). Still she was good at reading the price tags on things... So even her stint behind bars wouldn't bring her kudos or fame and she cried once again into a grey, limp, soggy tissue.

The rest of the session was a blur. The old judge stamped and raged after sentencing, the police on duty switched on the court TV to watch football, the jury had tea and coffee and Jimmelta was left to her own devices to get herself to Blackpool with the help of MOTO Mouth. She couldn't believe how her life was disappearing in front of her eyes. All she really wanted was a bath, real soap and a hot cup of tea. She never wanted to see a doughnut again. And there she was on national television, without lipstick or eye shadow in sight!

Outside the court she waited on the steps, shuffling from one foot to the other. She wondered about her family – Piggers and Dotty – and as it started to rain she wished she'd had the sense to wear a coat and sensible shoes. Nobody really cared about her, in or out of Bullion Castle, nobody phoned her, not even for the wrong number, nobody wanted her. Just as she was beginning to feel sorry for herself, a car sped to the bottom of the steps with its horn bellowing, grinding to a halt. Out of the passenger seat stepped a small man smoking a fat cigar. He looked like a football he was so round – it was difficult to see where his arms and legs started and finished. He ushered Jimmelta to the car between huge swirling puffs of smoke and pulled out a bag, offering her a doughnut. So there it was. She was being taken to her punishment by a small, fat agent who worked with MOTO Mouth.

'Tareque Sly's the name. I am the man MOTO Mouth has sent to help with the publicity and shows…' To Jimmelta this didn't seem to be making much sense. Her life was in shreds, her family had abandoned her… and worse, in the public light she looked awful. Tareque told a confused Jimmelta about how he had the job of managing the publicity of all new talent to ensure that they got a good deal when signing contracts. She nodded numbly in places when he told her about the famous people he had helped on the road to stardom.

The journey to Blackpool was punctuated with smoke- hurried conversations about deals, frenetic phone calls between press, photo shoots and, of course, mountains of doughnuts. Jimmelta felt quite guilty as she continuously munched her way through forty-three custard and raspberry ones, each one reminding her of the terrible time in Soho Prison. Life would be perfect if only she could return to Bullion Castle.

It was late into the night when the car approached the outskirts of Blackpool, but you couldn't miss the 'Illuminations' as the sky was consumed with a blaze of electrical colour. This, dear reader, was all new to Jimmelta, who had never so much as stepped onto litter-ridden land, mixed with greasy, beer-guzzling, snot-infested people who smelt of stale chips and lard. Thankfully, Tareque Sly was about to change that.

It was his dream to have a community reality programme with offenders being the new bait for the public, who would decide the tasks and punishments for each new convict. And, of course, Jimmelta was to be the sad, downtrodden soul who would be the new pawn! After quick negotiations with a TV station (incidentally, owned by Piggers), Sly had put together a presenter to monitor Jimmelta's daily progress; a series of activities to do each day; a couple of photo shoots with bands and magazines; and an in-depth interview with the manager, Reggie.

Having concocted a plan for the presenter of the reality series Big Toad, Little Slug to meet the sugar-faced Jimmelta on arrival, Sly decided whilst they were on air, that she should play, 'Who Wants To Be A Good Mother Then?' and she would answer questions about anything. Every time she got the correct answer, she could phone a child, but the wrong answer meant she would be given a household chore to do. Tareque was delighted and the presenter, Snailetta Bottom, a perfect choice for the first publicity shot, would trail Jimmelta every day reporting her activities to the public.

Heaving herself out of the limousine, Jimmelta was greeted by northern rain, gusts of coastline wind and blaring combinations of music which reverberated around the fairground. Rubbing her eyes and patting her straggly unkempt hair, she tried to give the image of sophistication. However, this was spoilt by the remains of doughnuts, sugar and jam on her once exclusive clothes. Squinting at the bright lights and flash bulbs, Jimmelta could see the outlines of figures looming towards her with microphones and as she gave a huge yawn, she was grabbed by the arm and ushered into an enclosure which reeked of fish and chips.

Did I mention that once Tareque had left London with Jimmelta, he had made long phone calls to someone about maximising the community service and making it a national sport? Desperate to get some rest after the horrible events back in court, our lovely convict fell asleep and was completely unaware of her fate as the one and only contestant for 'Community Reality.' This was to be headed by an overbearing determined and selfish commentator called Snailetta Bottom.

'Jimmelta, I am Snailetta Bottom, your host and reality presenter for the next sixty days! WELCOME!' In front of her was a tall willowy woman with black hair, blue eyes, spotty skin and the biggest nose that arched in a hoop down to her chin. Rather than this being seen as a deformity, her unusual feature was promoted by MOTO Mouth as an extraordinary feat of human nature, which the public loved. So Snailetta Bottom, once known as Tracey Smith, was now the nation's favourite presenter for the strange or absurd reality. Dear reader, there are times when we all must feel so grateful to be ordinary – not rich, famous or important, but when being a nonentity is such a luxury. How glad we are that we don't live in a gold castle, have a fetish for doughnuts, treat people badly and have no understanding of what makes the world go round. As we look down on Jimmelta dear

reader, and as we watch and track her continuing agony for the next sixty days, surrounded by greedy, odd, rather grotesque characters all wanting to make a quick buck out of her situation, let us be delighted and thrilled for the simple things in life.

'So Jimmelta, in front of this diverse audience, do you want to tell us about it? What happened? How did a lady surrounded by gold, who is best friends with Dotty, who lives in a castle, who has shoes etched in hand-picked black diamonds, whose social list includes some of the best known people; how did it get to this? THIS IS WHAT THE NATION WANTS TO KNOW!' Snailetta's well-discussed nose wiggled at the end as the rest of her face smiled and faced the TV cameras. In the background the fair cheered and clapped, whistles and yells of approval followed every statement. Snailetta, the public's darling, was gathering momentum. As the crowd roared, for a moment in the euphoria nothing mattered – except that Jimmelta badly needed the bathroom and there wasn't one in sight. She stood in the throng of the crowd with a beak-nosed half-witted celebrity presenter, cold, wet from the rain and in need of a hot bath. She began to cry – all this tragedy over a doughnut.

'You OK babe?' whispered Tareque, holding her by the elbow. She replied amidst the chaos and he suddenly roared like a protective lion caring for its cub, 'OUT OF THE WAY, ENOUGH QUESTIONS! SNAILETTA, YOU CAN START TOMORROW!

THE LADY NEEDS SOME LOOKING AFTER.'
The place went quiet and Jimmelta was ushered
to a building, taken to bathe, shower and to sleep
in a small make-shift bed. Being so exhausted and
thrilled she didn't even question the bed sheets. She
was grateful for the bath, soap and fresh towel. After
hot tea in a chipped and stained mug, she snuggled
down in to the bed, oblivious to everything, and fell
asleep. The damp, wet walls seemed wonderful to
her, the bath with real soap was a distant reminder
of a former, warmer and much cleaner life. Still,
our lovely Jimmelta was so delighted at the warmth.
Nothing mattered, her mind went blank and all her
cares disappeared.

Outside, the place was still buzzing with activity and
many people were curious as television equipment
and seating was erected at strategic places, some not
quite sure what the commotion was and who was
causing it. From behind the stalls, the fairground
people rubbed their hands in delight at the prospect
of being on national television and making a load
of money from the publicity. As the night wore on,
the crowds thinned out, leaving just a hard core of
reality followers (a bit like football supporters, but
committed to rubbish reality programmes) who
decided to camp outside the grounds in preparation
for the forthcoming events.

And as Jimmelta slept into the night, Snailetta,
Tareque and Reggie planned the activities and tasks
for the next sixty days, so that the public could be
entertained – at Jimmelta's emotional and physical
expense.

CHAPTER TWENTY

She woke to the sound of clanging, crashing, men shouting, arguing. And she woke to more northern rain. Trying to recall the bizarre events of the previous day was difficult. The judge, this strange man MOTO Mouth, Blackpool Illuminations, Tareque Sly and Snailetta Bottom... Jimmelta was so confused and tired she went back to sleep. It was the banging on the door that broke her slumber – and opening it slowly to see who it was, Jimmelta recognised the end of the beak.

'So Jimmelta, a new day in the fairground, how are you?'

Snailetta purred sweetly, as she saw a dishevelled untidy and yawning triangular slob nodding at her greetings. 'First things first. After getting ready, we have to introduce you to Reggie the manager: he'll tell you what stall you'll be working on today. After that, we'll stick you in with a few lions to show the public just how dangerous it can be. After that, there's a photo shoot with Snake Spin Slack, the hottest band of today.'

127

'After lunch you will be filmed mucking out the elephants – the kids will love it. Reggie will have an interview to say how you are settling into the new role. Oh, at four there's a phone-in from kids as you're on TV, so they can ask you about anything. AND THEN… we'll play "Who Wants To Be A Good Mother?" I'll tell you the rules later… this is going to be BRILLIANT. See you later!'

Snailetta spun out of the makeshift bedroom, leaving an even more confused and mentally exhausted Jimmelta.

Realising she had no clean clothes, Jimmelta tried to rub the dirt off her existing clothes. This as you can imagine was done very badly as other people had always done these tasks before. Suddenly the door flew open and she was flung some T-shirts, a huge shirt, underwear, massive denim dungarees, socks and hob-nailed boots.

'Get ready, have a bath and be down at Reggie's as quick as you can,' said a voice from the other side of the door, which promptly disappeared.

Twenty minutes later Jimmelta made her way through the maze of stalls and amusements to find Reggie, unaware that the nation was tracking her every movement, or that fashion critics were analysing the new attire and what it represented. Feeling more like something out of a freak show as the stall holders stared in bemusement and scorned her, she appeared ready to start her community service. She smiled and nodded – maybe this was what being Royal was like. Little did she know, however, that the whole country was following her demise and sentence avidly, many placing bets doubting whether she'd last the day, let alone the next sixty. This had also passed through Jimmelta's mind as she trudged through the sloppy knee-high mess left after the animals had started their day.

Reggie was a tall, bald, skinny man with a long, curling moustache and was only interested in money-making. He had a reputation for being quite cruel to his team and often refused to pay wages if stall holders caused trouble. He liked nothing more than getting the most out of his staff and animals and never bothered about the upkeep of the amusements. However, he liked new ideas and would buy the oddest rides or activities to draw the punter into his grounds. Reggie knew he was going to hate Jimmelta, if only because she was disgustingly rich and lived in the Strand in a castle made purely out of gold. He was going to get the public on his side, get some of her money and become famous – simple!

'Well well well. We don't normally get your sort up this way, more the posh places in London; still a little bit of hard work won't 'arm anyone will it?' he said as his opening statement to a worried Jimmelta, who once again just nodded. Anything for peace.

'Well lady, your job is to muck out all the animals all day and pick up the litter. After a week of doin' that we'll see if you're ready for something more challenging. I gather you've got MOTO Mouth as a PR guy? Now, I'll be wanting a cut of the profits – I'm thinking sixty-forty to me since I've saved you from jail. I'll also be deciding which photo shoots you do. 'Course they'll be another cut for me. So, Chew whatever-your-name is, we're all happy. By the way, keep that long-beaked, spotty monster away from me. Snailetta Bottom, I won't get anything from 'er.'

'Such a charming man,' oozed Jimmelta to the cameras. She was determined to get through this with doughnuts and dignity.

'Snailetta, have you thought of running a profile on Reggie as I am sure the viewers would love to see how he cares for everything?' The reporter agreed, knowing along with the nation what had already taken place in the first meeting.

After all the events and shoots with the band, Jimmelta played "Who Wants To Be A Good Mother Then?"

'So, Jimmelta, first day over. Still feeling good? Excellent. Here's the question: Do you make 'Yorkshire Puddings' with a) stone b) heather c) eggs, or d) flowers? DIFFICULT out of Yorkshire! The crowd is with you. Hello to all viewers… What's the answer?' The camera crew, stall holders, Reggie and even the animals went quiet as they leaned forward for the answer. Scratching the nits in her hair, Jimmelta tried to remember if she had ever seen the Inherited Australian Convicts make them. Her mother hadn't – she didn't know what the kitchen looked like. Nobody ate stone, she mused as she picked hardened pooh off her dungarees, and flowers didn't taste nice at all, unless you were Chinese. Since she was a founder member of the Church of Harvey Nichols, anything to do with food that was up-and-coming, she would know about. No, heather was out, this only left eggs. Eggs it was.

'Eggs, Snailetta, eggs.' A roar of applause filled the showground. She smiled and thought of her bath tonight, a cleanish towel and soap... and a talk with her family. Only fifty-nine more days of this. She was determined that this was going to be a success.

CHAPTER TWENTY ONE

The phone line to Bullion Castle was engaged. Well, the truth was, it was off the hook. The Inherited Australian Convicts had been resting – again – and Rooster saw MOTO Mouth give an interview on national news, saying this was the first time reality shows were involved in community service, working closely with law and order. His jaw dropped when he saw footage of Jimmelta arriving with Tareque Sly at the Blackpool Illuminations, dirty, messy, crumpled and probably smelly. Not wanting to upset the children who were now happily into their chores before and after school, he managed to find One-Eared Lumpy and show him the news about Fat Doughy. Instead of laughing at her ridiculous situation, One-Eared Lumpy said, 'I never wanted it to go this far Rooster. Shall we rescue her and bring her back to Bullion? Looks to me as if she has learnt her lesson and I don't think the kids should see her like this.' Rooster nodded. Enough was enough, perhaps they could persuade the judge to let her to finish her community service back at Bullion Castle.

'Let's get rid of the TVs and put them in the golden loft so the kids don't get upset. It'll be awful if they see 'er like this,' commented One-Eared Lumpy, feeling guilty at Jimmelta's humiliation and distress. He knew how she liked to be clean and beautifully dressed, even if she was a fat doughy. Somehow, the interview with Snailetta Bottom and MOTO Mouth made her into a victim being persecuted, rather than a criminal doing sentence. As the cameras scanned her clothes it was obvious the remains of her designer stuff had gone and now Jimmelta looked like a labourer on a building site ready to mix cement.

'Let's keep the kids sorted. Gingham's cooking tonight, some new Italian recipe; Polka's gardening and sortin' out the herbs. Then there's Paisley, he's still on school report for not getting' 'omework in on time. So we'll move the TVs and the phones.'

Strangely enough, as the chores mounted up in the house for the children, they each had begun to enjoy taking pride in their duties, all under the impression that their mother was on holiday with Piggers in some South American country. Things had certainly changed. Gingham had found a new desire to cook and often prepared the main meal in the evening for everyone to eat. So the Inherited Australian Convicts were now learning new table manners as they joined the four children for dinner, on the condition they ate and spoke properly. In return, the children were expected to prepare the food and clean and tidy it away.

So it came to pass, dear reader, that the new, now no longer enforced, regime made living and working easier in Bullion Castle. No longer did the convicts hate the children or despise their untold affluence. In fact, as the days progressed, a respect between them all developed. Polka missed her mother and Kidston mentioned her all the time, but the Inherited Australian Convicts had a series of little white lies to stop them worrying. However, even they had not expected Jimmelta to stay away quite so long and in their quieter moments they were concerned. Though in a sarcastic moment, they thought she might have discovered a doughnut mountain in an eastern bloc country.

Never in a million years or in the Church of Harvey Nichols had they expected her to be doing community service at Blackpool Illuminations. They shuddered at the thought of the cruel northern winds, especially being Australian and used to hot weather.

CHAPTER TWENTY TWO

E ach day brought new horrors for Jimmelta, over and above mucking out the animals, oiling the machinery, collecting the litter from each stall and getting rid of the rubbish. Reggie relished their morning meetings as his list grew each day and the public sent in their votes to Snailetta, responding to the activities.

Reggie was determined to make the most of his new-found fame and bought a new checked jacket in red, green and gold. The grey hair was no more: he invested in a private hairdresser to dye his fading locks and moustache a deep dark black, to create this new sophisticated image. He made sure that his office had fresh flowers each day for when the cameras starting rolling and found a cheap air spray on offer to use in the interviews.

The path leading up to his sooty and industrial office was now edged in daffodils and heather, all to be paid for by the taxpayer. When interviewed with Snailetta, he used the new flowery cups and saucers from Pound and Pence with a mock china finish and ditched the family packets of broken custard creams, replacing them with Hob Nobs – quite an apt choice.

Of course, whilst the lavish Reggie and Snailetta played their best side to the public, Jimmelta had to wear the same worn, dirt-infested clothes, her hair gathering grease by the day along with her ever-growing spots. However, dear reader, as we know, the public always loves a loser, someone down and out, someone who gives human nature no hope at all. So let's see if this might be the saving of our very lovely Jimmelta. Read on and find out, but dear reader, don't give your sympathy too easily...

As the days progressed Jimmelta grew so tired, she didn't even try to outwit the loathsome Snailetta Bottom, Tareque Sly or Reggie. She was too tired to eat, wash or change her clothes. Meanwhile, the cunning Snailetta's wardrobe became so dazzling that the daily papers had likened her to a new fashion icon whose attire caused a sensation everywhere. And, of course, she was delighted that her contestant's clothes were becoming increasingly dirty, dank and disgusting. This was not the Chew Van Der Bratt seen only in the best shops or at social events. Now, luxury to Jimmelta was having a clean mug to drink her cold mouldy tea from, or sheets of plastic to shield her from the sleet and rain as she completed her tasks. However, in her quieter moments she was scathing about the working conditions and vowed to punish Snailetta, Reggie and Tareque once she was home in Bullion Castle. There wasn't much she wasn't going to do to them!

'Community Reality' had built up enormous momentum with the public as not only was it was entertaining, but moreover it was the morality tale in action. The people loved it. Jimmelta had gone from being presented as a fat blubbering lump of outrageously spoilt flesh, whom the public despised because of her unquenchable thirst a n d greed for opulence, to a wizened, dirty, muck-raking zombie. But, dear reader, did I say WIZENED?

Indeed, the most amazing transformation was taking place. Too tired to eat and hating the three dollops of food each day, Jimmelta's appetite slowly diminished as all she wanted to do was sleep. The Illuminations heaved each day to breaking point, as the public swarmed and paid to get a glimpse of their contestant in her habitat, whilst Reggie was making a load of money. Snailetta and Tareque handled the publicity because Chew Van Der Bratt was now becoming a bit of a brand. But dear reader, Jimmelta was unaware of this as she wasn't allowed to watch television, and, therefore, had no idea of the magnitude of her fame.

We could go on about the injustice she had to endure, but you must remember why she had ended up scraping chewing gum off toilet seats and sick off stalls. Her insatiable greed for doughnuts – and her inability to avoid being selfish towards others. So there we have it, once a mother who spent her life ordering the Inherited Australian Convicts in Bullion Castle, she was now being made to complete the most menial and humiliating tasks in front of a huge public each day on TV.

Her dungarees seemed to be even baggier as the weeks progressed. Not being able to get through to her children and family had made Jimmelta so distraught. Food was the last thing on her mind. And the drudgery of each day would have continued if it hadn't been for the Inherited Australian Convicts who, although they could be disparaging about 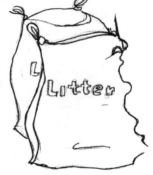 their mistress, now felt she had served more than enough time at Blackpool Illuminations.

'We 'ave to do something men,' muttered Rooster as he switched off the TV. She's done her time – let's get her out.'

'But what can we do? We ain't got any power and Pigger's not back yet...' replied One-Eared Lumpy, tidying the dishes away in the kitchen.

'I know who we will ask,' said Pinky Squat, pointing at Buckingham Palace. 'Her! Dotty an' her are good friends…'

'Naw she ain't allowed to interfere with the law. She can do nothing. Let's get the PM to stop these shows as it makes a mockery of the law…' declared Rooster, quite pleased with the solution. 'This ain't right. Only we 'ave the right to make it difficult for 'er' he added, concerned at the latest footage of Jimmelta looking dazed and dizzy as she filled her thirtieth bag of litter. The phone line was jammed with members of the public giving their vote on how hard she was working. The final calls and percentages would determine how much lunch she was allowed.

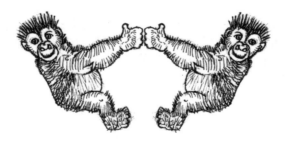

Unbeknown to Jimmelta, her scouring and cleaning tactics were now making national news, especially when she scoured out the baby gorillas' cages, crying as they hadn't been cared for in weeks. The nation cried with her when she gave the youngest one her only mouldy biscuits and spent the time stroking and talking to them. Soon Sooty and Sweep became the nation's favourite gorillas.

Strange things were happening, dear reader – all unexpected and quite moving; the more successful and harsh Snailetta appeared, the less the public liked her; the more Jimmelta swayed, fainted and worked into the night, especially cleaning and caring for the animals, the more the public loved her and demanded her release. The fly-on-the-wall documentary designed to make her look spoilt, selfish and utterly revolting, reflected a once repugnant lady who now was prepared to forgo her meals so that the animals encaged in the theme park could have a little more food.

The main news anchor story showed a petition signed by millions of children across the country demanding her release, followed by the arrest of Reggie, who had become decidedly nervous as his popularity plummeted. Perhaps one of the most interesting facts to emerge was the lack of desire for doughnuts, gold and diamond shoes by Jimmelta, who saw her waistline diminishing daily. In fact, such was the interest in her weight loss that the Chew Van Der Bratt was now a reference to housewives everywhere for making housework the new health regime! Of course, you and I know the truth; Jimmelta was fat and simply ate too much. But by not eating doughnuts and living on cold mouldy food, followed by tough activities and tasks set by Snailetta and others, she would lose weight. So, "doing a Chew Van Der Bratt" epitomizing drastic weight loss, meant you lived a life of slavery, or that you were changing your greedy, self-centred ways!

And still Jimmelta had no idea of her fame, reducing waistband or her increasing national popularity. She was too busy cleaning up after the animals in Blackpool Illuminations. That said, she was often puzzled at the amount of customers who asked for her autograph in between tasks, smiling and waving as she worked. Occasionally, a child would touch her dust pan and brush, or her bin liner full of litter and rubbish. She thought this was strange, rather odd. Nobody, she noticed, came forward to help her – not once – and this she found even more strange.

She wondered if her life could be any stranger, or get any stranger.

Students in secondary schools used 'Community Reality' in debates as all had strong views on the principles of punishment and felt that this form of slavery over a doughnut was like something out of the middle ages. Such was the anger about Jimmelta's working conditions by the public that several MPs mentioned it in Downing Street at cabinet level with other members of the government. And like all political establishments, the government responded slowly, unaware of the rage people felt about the conditions for Jimmelta and her beloved animals. Finally, a press release was issued by the government saying that in this day and age in the western world, justice had to be seen to have been done. Jimmelta had paid the price and should now be freed.

'On behalf of the PM, I, his press secretary, Pretentious Pinchingthorpe-Munching-Mop-Phillips, would like to issue a statement in response to the petition for the release of Jimmelta Chew Van Der Bratt from community service at Blackpool Illuminations...' Ah dear reader, you probably recognise the surname. Pretentious was the noble brother of the ignoble Precarious, who, as we know, manipulated parents and children alike. I should mention at this point that Precarious Pinchingthorpe-Munching-Mop-Phillips had cashed in on Jimmelta's horrific fall from grace and sudden rise to stardom by selling Chew Van Der Bratt T-shirts and exercise tapes at the school gates. Not one to miss an opportunity, he would only allow students to play and have a break if they bought one of his "Rescue Jimmelta!" ties (in different colours for each day of the week). Such was the fame of the non-educational school as a result of poor Jimmelta's exposure on TV, that Precarious managed to get a small ten-minute slot nationally called "A Conversation with Our Colleagues... Issues of Today". And whilst his ratings were not really that good, Precarious had to admit he was the best looking 'Child Innovator' around. Well that's what some of his fans said!

Of course, nobody knew that it was he who had contacted MOTO Mouth and Snailetta Bottom, enticing them both with dreams of even more fame and money. But dear reader, don't ask me how this little man knew – I can only suggest that due to his underhand ways, he made it his business to be involved in everything which didn't concern him.

As the statement was read, millions of people up and down the country stopped whatever they were doing and cheered. Over the weeks they had become very fond of Jimmelta.

Clearing his throat, Pretentious smoothed his grey hair back off his face, wiped his thick-rimmed glasses with his old and shabby tie and, after quickly glancing at the photographers all squeezing to get a good view, looked ahead straight into the camera.

'We, the government, feel that devising a reality programme centred around the sentences carried out by defendants is totally horrifying. It sends out the message that being convicted of a minor crime is an opportunity to court fame. We are horrified that well-known public relations companies such as Grabba and Dosha should be promoting, praising and profiteering from anti-social and illegal behaviour. It is to the discredit of this company and the public characters associated with it, namely MOTO Mouth, Tareque Sly and Snailetta Bottom, that the government has been forced to take action to create new legislation:

This will protect the principles of justice.

This will allow minor offences to be treated severely in the correct manner – even if a doughnut is involved.

This will make people or companies intent on profiteering from criminal doings one of the most penalised sections of the community.

Therefore, it has been decided, along with twenty-four million voters, that Jimmelta Chew Van Der Bratt should terminate her community service and return to her "humble abode". All the people involved in gaining from her misfortune will be arrested and sent immediately to jail for life and a half. The judge passing the original verdict has previously been labelled as mad as a hatter, so the sentence is null and void...'

The small speckled-faced man flicked his slick greasy hair back off his face. There the viewers saw an evil twinkle in his eyes as he spoke in disgust about the money-spinners.

CHAPTER TWENTY THREE

The cameras spun back to Blackpool where the country watched Reggie being handcuffed, dragged through litter and slung into a police van. One policeman carried his convict's bulging suitcase, laden with money for each day of the reality community programme, whilst Reggie roared out that the money had been 'given in good faith'. As he bellowed and stamped his feet, his greasy, spotty, sallow face turned into a deep purple rage, and one by one his blackheads and spots exploded on to those nearby. Now, not only was he a disgustingly, cruel, greedy and an underhand person, he was also vile and repugnant to look at. The pus from the large bulbous mounds squirted at the policeman. Quickly, so as not to cause any commotion, the officers took a dirty old wax cover, used to keep the animals warm, and slung it over Reggie. As he was thrown into the van with the sirens on full blast, the crowds of reporters turned their attention to the next victim.

Slumping against the door of the office, looking dishevelled, eye makeup running down the long hook-like nose, the nation's not-so-favourite presenter was howling into her expensive cape, whilst nearby

Jimmelta

The Servants

Precarious Pinchingthorpe-Munching-Mop-Phillips

Tareque Sly

Snailetta Bottom

165

Reggie

Grandfather Tuttersmat

**Grandfather Splutterap
& his Wife**

PC Clacker-Hammer

Policemen

Female Inmate

The Judge

AUTHOR PROFILE

Have you always written?

Yes, but I never had the time to sit down and do it and enjoy it. Teaching is jolly hard and exhausting though VERY rewarding.

Where do you write?

Somewhere comfortable, with a cup of tea and lots of jumpers, generally my husband's or son's – so I am warm!

How do you think of your story?

Well with a young adult's story, I tend to think or devise the name so the characters start to form, along with the story-line. With adult literature it's different. I tend to have an idea and work from there.

What's your earliest memory of writing?

Writing in my garden as a little girl, and reading the made

up stories to my dog Snowy, who strangely didn't understand a thing!

Do you like your characters?

Characters are like people. They develop, have strengths and weaknesses and, as the writer, I like them to take their own paths and develop their personalities in the story. Some, like Jimmelta, start off revolting, but become quite decent. Others, like

Precarious Pinchingthorpe-Munching-Mop-Phillips
and Snailetta, always stay quite horrible. I wouldn't
want to meet them!

How do you write?

I write through episodes or events rather than
numbers of words. So when there is a stumbling
block about what to do next, I think it through until
it sits right in my mind.

What do you see when you write?

I think all writers see their stories differently. When
writing
young adult books I see caricatures and large actions,
generally lots of colours and extreme detail. I tend to
imagine teenagers describing things so, I try to give
that sort of picture.

Do your books have messages?

Every book has some type of message. I think this
one shows the vulgarity of people, with lessons to be
taught, and a form of redemption – good conquering
bad. However, it is intended to be fun!!

How do you know when you have finished?

How do you know when to leave a conversation or
say good bye to a friend? You just do.

Who is your inspiration to write?

My father, a very clever and most creative man who
has always composed and has had lots of works
published, and is the most brilliantly positive person
I know. You always need somebody like that – even
if it's for your homework.

What do you have to learn to enjoy about writing?

When you write, you must learn to love checking, editing, starting again, and finding the right words to use in your story. You know when it's right.

So what should I do?

Enjoy this book, laugh and have fun.

Then what?

Go back into the class room and knock the socks off your teacher and write to entertain your audience. And have fun!!

Any advice?

Don't buy a golden table! You'll spend all your creative time polishing!!

Author visits and workshops in schools

Become an author for a day!!

Anne is available for author visits to schools which are stimulating, and using her expertise in literacy and education supplies a package that is not only challenging and innovative, but can help to improve writing back in the classroom.

Resources linked to the curriculum are made to cater for each class/group, so afterwards can be used as a tool to support literacy at KS1, KS2, KS3.

Fun days with lots of excitement which also develop writing and literacy skills.

A variety of packages available to suit needs, enjoyment and of course, budget.

Contact:

Email: annestairmandj@hotmail.co.uk

Telephone number: 01206 273175